AIRSHIP 27 PRODUCTIONS

Behowls the Moon
© 2019 Philip McCormac

Published by Airship 27 Productions
www.airship27.com
www.airship27hangar.com

Interior illustrations © 2019 Rob Davis
Cover illustration © 2019 Steve Otis

Editor: Ron Fortier
Associate Editor: Gordon Dymowski
Marketing and Promotions Manager: Michael Vance
Production and design by Rob Davis

ISBN-13: 978-1-946183-66-8
ISBN-10: 1-946183-66-0

Printed in the United States of America

10 9 8 7 6 5 4 3 2 1

by Philip McCormac

Now the hungry lion roars,
And the wolf behowls the moon;
Whilst the heavy ploughman snores,
All with weary task fordone.

– *William Shakespeare*

A Midsummer Night's Dream, Act 5, Scene 1.

CHAPTER ONE

"That Aishling is a wild woman," Raurí Mac Cathail marvelled out loud. The youngster gingerly fingered the bite in his neck. "She must have bit me in the passion of the moment and I never noticed." In spite of the soreness of the wound, Raurí chortled. "At least I think it must have been Aishling—unless it was a flea, but it would take a hell of a big flea to make that kind of bite."

Abruptly Raurí stopped walking and peered at the sinister forms on the road up ahead. He felt decidedly uneasy and some of his cheerfulness evaporated into the chill of the night. Up until then he had been feeling pretty pleased with the evening's merriment and with good reason, for he had managed to isolate Aishling O'Hagan from the formidable Benedict Phelan and lure her outside.

The young woman had arrived only recently in the district and was staying with the widow, Ina Riley. It was said the widow was cursed—or some might think blessed—with the third eye. It was commonly believed she had powers beyond the ordinary world and people went to her for cures and charms.

Raurí and Aishling had sneaked behind the byre where he had an enjoyable time exploring the voluptuous body of the young woman. But then something strange happened. It was almost as if Aishling had taken over and was leading Raurí in the lovemaking.

He had memory of Aishling tearing at his clothes, with an animal-like ferocity and the small growls of pleasure as they made love. No woman Raurí had ever been with had behaved in such a manner. It bothered him a little as he relived the experience. Sometime during that ecstasy of passion Aishling must have bitten him.

He recalled the venomous look on Benedict Phelan's face, when he saw Raurí and Aishling wander back into the *ceilidh,* arm in arm. Phelan had been the bane of Raurí's life since their schooldays. The bully lost no opportunity to harass the younger boy. Tonight was not the first time Raurí had snatched a female from under the nose of his rival. Raurí walked on towards the men, gingerly fingering the wound in his neck.

"Halloa!" he called, but there was no response. "Fine night to be out under the stars."

Raurí kept walking, his pace slowing as his apprehension grew. And then he stopped. What was he to do? He could turn and run back down the lane. And then that option was closed as he heard a noise behind and he turned to see two men emerge on the footpath behind him.

"Phelan... is that you Benedict? What's going on?"

And Raurí suddenly had an idea what was coming.

"It's about Aishling O'Hagan, you bastard. You were with her."

"What? Where's the harm in that?"

"I saw her first. I had my eye on her. Then you had to interfere. You're a menace to decent women, Mac Cathail. We know your reputation."

Raurí had an air of youthful innocence which proved irresistible to the opposite sex—some wanting passionately to make love to him, while arousing in others a desire to mother him. Whatever the attraction, Raurí had a habit of turning it to his own advantage.

But Benedict Phelan obviously wasn't too pleased that Raurí had supplanted him in the courting game. The big man was waiting to kick the stuffing out of him. There were a few unsolved murders in the district. Phelan was a prime suspect but nothing could ever be pinned on him. People were scared of the Phelan family and what would happen if they came forward to bear witness.

Raurí looked beyond Benedict and saw his equally big and brutal brother, Dermot, grinning in cruel anticipation of the fun to come. Then there were the two men behind—a quartet of big brutes out to put Raurí Mac Cathail in the bog.

It looked like Raurí would have to fight for his life. Raurí could fight all right, but he doubted if he could get the better of these hulking gombeens. Benedict raised a great shovel-like hand and beckoned.

"Come Raurí, We just need to slap you around a wee bit. Rearrange that baby face of yours. You'll not be so pretty when we finish. Maybe the next girl you look at will think twice about letting you near her. Come now. We can't wait all night. It'll be dawn soon. Come on and take your medicine like a man."

Phelan reached out and pushed Raurí in the chest, making the youngster stumble back. Raurí cringed, trying to look scared which wasn't difficult.

"Please, don't," he whined. "I'm sorry."

Phelan grinned as he made a fist of one hand and ground it into the palm of the other; that massive fist, as big as a mallet and of the same consistency, ready to smash this gutless creature into the turf.

"Come now, Raurí. You know you have sinned. I am your saviour. When we have finished you'll sin no more."

Raurí moved swiftly and kicked Phelan in the bollix. There was a wheezing grunt and the big man folded over. Raurí had his hand in Phelan's hair pulling him further down as he smashed his knee into Benedict's face. Keeping his grip in that mop of greasy hair, Raurí powered forward using the injured man like a battering ram and driving him into his retarded brother.

Two hundred and eighty pounds of muscle and flesh propelled backwards was an irresistible force and Dermot bleated like a frightened sheep when his brother cannoned into him. As Benedict went down Raurí punched hard into the thick neck. Benedict Phelan hit the road with a slam that knocked the breath from him. He lay on his back gasping like a landed fish and just as helpless.

Dermot reacted much faster than Raurí anticipated. He swung his cudgel, aiming for Raurí's head. Raurí might have dodged the blow if Benedict had not reached out and grabbed his ankle. The crude club scraped down Raurí's ear and bounced off his shoulder. Raurí yelled and tried to kick Benedict in the head. But with his ankle held fast he could not quite bring it off and then his foot was yanked so forcefully Raurí overbalanced and went down. Dermot was swinging again with his crude weapon. Raurí brought up his arm to protect himself and felt piercing agony as his forearm took the full force of the blow.

Squirming with pain, Raurí could hear the slap of feet as the rearguard pounded up to join in the attack. He rolled desperately towards the side of the lane. A boot thudded into his ribs. As he curled up in agony something hard cracked into the side of his head. Coloured lights flashed across his vision. Dermot Phelan raised his nail-studded club and hit the youth again and again. Raurí tried to cry out but a boot thudded into his mouth.

By the time Benedict got to his feet to join in the attack the battered youngster was too far gone to feel anything. The boots thudded into his unresisting body. The crude cudgel pounded his unfeeling flesh until his assailants grew tired. They left off and stood panting and breathless.

"Is he dead?"

"If he ain't dead then he's damn near it."

"The bastard won't mess around with any more women. Throw him in the bog. Then we better be long gone before anyone comes along."

CHAPTER TWO

Among the inhabitants of Carrybeg was a much reviled orphan, Damian Hughes. Damian had two things going against him. He was been born out of wedlock and with certain abnormalities. Subsequently the locals shunned him, the way ignorant folk do. Sometime in the past, Raurí had come upon a group of men abusing Damian and had taken the outcast's part. Damian was immensely strong with thick muscular arms and shoulders, but he had always cringed away from his tormentors, not able to retaliate. When Raurí came to his aid, something ignited within Damian. He leapt into the fray and fought alongside Raurí. In the resulting fight, the pair put the abusers to flight.

That day changed everything for Damian. He discovered, because he fought back, people got into the habit of crossing to the opposite side of the road when they saw him approach. From that day also, Damian fell in love with the young god who had come to his rescue, though never by word or gesture did he give hint of his infatuation. For his part Raurí accepted the friendship without asking for anything in return.

On the fateful night Raurí was kicked into oblivion, Damian, hoping to meet up with his idol, arrived as the fight was ending. Unaware of the identity of the victim, Damian could empathise with the poor wretch who was being beaten, for in the past, before Raurí showed him different, he had been the butt end of such hidings. Damian watched as the lifeless body was rolled into the bog where he knew it would eventually sink into the mire.

Damian wanted to ascertain the identity of the victim. Such information might come in useful. As soon as the gang departed Damian crept forward, scanning the lane both ways. He knew he was taking a risk. If he were found in the vicinity of the dead body he would be accused of the killing. Damian stopped by the ditch and peered down at the motionless figure.

If anyone had heard the cry that emerged from the throat of that lonely creature, they would have imagined some animal in extreme agony or, as this was the Ireland of 1916, a creature from the otherworld of the *sidhe*.

Damian thought his heart would burst inside his chest when he saw the inert figure of his idol in the stinking mire of the bog. Mewling pitifully he crouched down and reached out to touch the battered face of the one person he loved above his own life.

"Raurí, my beautiful Raurí."

Tears flowed unchecked down Damian's weather-beaten cheeks.

"What have they done to you, my beautiful boy? Oh, Rauri, Rauri, Rauri!"

The outcast raised his fist and shook it in the air.

"I will avenge you. I will avenge this dreadful crime. Phelan, you are a dead man walking, for I will not rest until you join poor Rauri in the bog."

Damian realized he could not leave his friend to lie abandoned in this cold and lonely grave. He crouched on the road and reaching out, tenderly stroked Rauri's face, then gripped his jacket and hauled the body back into the lane, sobbing as he did so. For someone of his immense strength it was not a problem recovering Rauri, who weighed at least one hundred and seventy pounds. Ignoring the blood and mud, Damian wrapped his arms around the body of his friend and hugging him close rocked back and forth as he knelt in the roadway.

"My beautiful Rauri,' he sobbed, and his tears dripped on the face of the only creature he had ever dared love. "My beautiful Rauri, what am I going to do without you? You beautiful, beautiful boy. They have killed you and I wasn't here to protect you. I will never rest until they have paid the price for this terrible crime." He raised his unprepossessing, tear-streaked face to the night sky. "Hear this, God, if there is such a thing!" he suddenly roared. "I swear on the body of this poor innocent and beautiful boy, I will slay every one of those foul creatures that killed my Rauri. I will kill their fathers and mothers and their brothers and sisters and their cousins and aunts and uncles. I shall wipe out the name of the Phelan clan from off the face of the earth."

After this outburst, he moaned pitifully and swayed back and forth, grief-stricken for the loss of the most precious person ever to enter his lonely, impoverished life. As he rocked he thought he heard a sigh and immediately ceased all movement.

"Rauri," he whispered, peering down at the face of the youth.

He put his ear against Rauri's lips, his own breath stopped within his throat. Slowly that ugly face was lifted to gaze out across the lightening sky as dawn stretched tenuous fingers across the bog.

"Dear God, Rauri, I believe there is breath still within you. Oh, dear God what am I to do? You are near death as it is. How can I drag you back into the world of the living?"

Damian clambered to his feet. He knew what had to be done. And it had to be done quickly before the full light of day cast its revealing rays across the world. Holding the precious bundle in his arms with all the tenderness of a lover he strode rapidly along, his eyes anxiously scouring the countryside for movement that might indicate people out and about. He knew Raurí must be spirited away if he was to stand any chance of surviving. If Phelan suspected his victim still lived or that there was a witness to the attempted murder, he would move quickly to silence them both.

There was one place where Raurí would be safe. It was also the place where he might stand a chance of being healed, if indeed it was not too late. Damian knew of one person who might have the skills to bring Raurí back from the brink of death. And so he scurried along the roads, the burden in his arms the most precious thing he had ever carried.

• • •

Ina Riley stirred the porridge in the iron pot simmering over the turf fire. She was thinking about her granddaughter, Aishling, when the young woman walked in the front door yawning widely.

"Well, you've decided to come home, at last." Ina observed. "How was the *ceilidh*? Did you meet anyone interesting?"

"Interesting around here—in this asshole of nowhere! They're all big thick men with big thick heads with porridge for brains."

"I hope you behaved yourself."

Aishling shrugged and made a pout.

"There was one young fellow I took a shine to. He was quite nice."

"You didn't do anything foolish."

"I can't remember. I got a bit carried away."

"For God's sake, Aishling, you'll have to be careful." Ina looked up frowning. "You didn't bite him or anything or make the change."

Aishling smiled dreamily.

"I might have nibbled him a little. But I don't think I broke the skin. At least I don't think so. I went a wee bit berserk for a time before I was able to assert control. He wouldn't have noticed anyway. He was full of poteen and lust—a deadly combination in the Irish."

The young woman giggled.

"Aishling, please be careful. I don't want to lose you." The older woman ceased her stirring and looked over at her granddaughter. "I promised your father I would look after you. At least living here with me, people won't bother you. I don't get many visitors and when I do they usually come under cover of darkness hoping no one will see them."

"You and your spells and potions." Again Aishling chuckled. "What do they ask for, anyway?"

"Usually it's young people wanting love potions; or older men wanting to rejuvenate their love life."

Ina turned back to the fire and resumed stirring. When she spoke again it was in a more sombre voice.

"Then there are the women with fruit ripening the womb. Married women and young girls, wanting rid of their lovechild. I try to talk them out of it but most of them are desperate and can see no other way."

"You sound sad, Grandma."

Ina swung the pot away from the fire. She ladled a portion of the steaming porridge into a bowl.

"You're sure you don't want some of this?"

"Yuk!"

Aishling stuck her fingers in her mouth and pretended to heave.

"All right, all right, I get the message."

"I brought back some rabbits," Aishling said. "You're welcome to share."

"I haven't your taste for raw flesh or even cooked flesh for that matter. Porridge and herrings suits this old body of mine just fine." Before Ina could sit there was a knock on the door. "It's always the same. Just when you're in the middle of something."

Grumbling, she went to answer.

"Damian Hughes, what on earth have you got there?"

"He's bad hurt, Ina. Can you help?"

"Come in."

Ina directed Damian to a dilapidated settee where he laid down his bundle. Ina examined the injured man, unbuttoning soaking muddy garments and running her hands over his body, noting swellings and ruptures. Aishling peered over her shoulder.

"It's him," she gasped.

"Get some blankets and warm them by the fire. Damian, give me a hand to get his clothes off. Who did this?"

"I... I don't know. I found him lying in a ditch. I didn't know what else to do so I brought him here"

If Ina noticed the tremor in Damian's voice she gave no indication. She probed the body, her fingers lingering over the bite in the youngster's neck.

"Will he... can you...?"

Damian stumbled to a halt and this time there was no mistaking the sob in his voice.

"We'll do our best. Aishling, bring those blankets. We need to keep him warm."

The women worked over the injured youngster, wrapping him in the blankets. Ina took his pulse and pulled back his eyelids looking for signs of brain damage. There was little or no response from Raurí. He lay like one dead and indeed his pallor was that of a corpse. Ina turned to Damian hovering nervously in the background.

"I will do what I can to save him. But he is near death as it is. I can't promise."

"Don't send me away, Ina. Let me stay."

The healer stared shrewdly at Damian, saw the anguish in his eyes and understood something of what this youngster meant to the outcast.

"Go in the back room. There's a bed there."

Damian shook his head and turned to the door.

"I'll wait outside."

Once he had left Ina turned to Aishling.

"Normal healing procedures won't save this one." Ina stared steadily into the eyes of the younger woman. "When Damian brought Raurí in you said it was him. What was that about?"

"I met him at the dance. He's the one I told you about."

"There's a bite on his neck. Unless his attacker did that I can only assume it was you. Aishling I need to know. Did you bite him?"

"I didn't mean to. Don't let him die, Grandma."

"He needs blood. Perhaps it was fortunate you did bite. You may have infected him, and a transfusion of your blood might just save him. If that doesn't work then he will surely die. Are you willing to help him?"

Aishling put out her hand and rested in on Raurí's cold forehead.

"For this is my blood," she intoned, "the blood of the new and enduring covenant which I will give onto you that you may share in the life of the ancient order."

CHAPTER THREE

When Raurí awoke he lay still, wondering where he was. The *ceilidh!* He had downed a lot of poteen. And then he had encountered Aishling! What a woman! Things were slotting into place.

Aishling O'Hagan! She was like no woman he had ever encountered. Was he in love with her? Raurí felt somewhat uneasy about that. Perhaps she was a little too forward. Pulling him down on top of her. Even now he felt himself reacting to the memory of her touch.

"Aishling," he murmured aloud.

Aishling was insatiable and exciting. Driving him to heights of ecstasy he had never believed possible. It was as if she had taken over his role and he was the one being seduced. Raurí sighed. He would like to see her again and that was certain.

Raurí stared up at the ceiling. It was vaulted affair with curved oaken beams crisscrossing and making oblique patterns against the plastered ceiling. He blinked. Where the hell was he?

A choir was singing. Abruptly he sat up and stared around him. He was in a church! Raurí stared in puzzlement at the rows of candles giving a muted illumination and leaving more of the chapel in shadow than in light. He noticed a priest dressed in dark vestments. The priest had his back to Raurí and was facing the altar. He raised his arms and in solemn voice crooned a phrase in Latin. The choir chanted their response. Raurí blinked. There was a religious service going on.

He had no memory of arriving at this place of worship. What day was it? It was Friday when he went to the *ceilidh*. Had he lost a day? What had happened to him on Saturday? Raurí could recall nothing after leaving the dance.

He glanced down at his body and with a shock realized he was naked. Raurí stared fearfully at the priest who just then turned and raised his arms.

"Lord of all things sublime, we are gathered here to pray for the soul of our dear brother, Raurí Mac Cathail."

"No," Raurí whispered. "I can't be dead."

With a great effort of will Raurí forced himself to clamber out of the coffin. He looked down at his nakedness noting how pale he was; almost ghostlike.

"No, I don't want to be dead."

Two young acolytes turned from the altar. They were swinging censors and the smoke drifted sinuously towards the naked youth like serpents released from confinement. Raurí stood mesmerised, watching the tendrils of smoke drift towards him. In his time, he had hunted badgers with dogs and it was this same earthy odour that came to him in the smoke. Instead of the sweet scent of frankincense he smelt trees and crushed pine needles and disturbed soil and animal musk.

"Where am I?" he yelled hoarsely.

And then he noticed the faces of acolytes. They were not little boys as he had imagined but had the faces of small beasts. Quickly he glanced up at the priest. The priest had the features of a dog. No wait, it wasn't a dog it was much more like that of a wild thing—a fox, or more like a... a wolf. And then Raurí knew he was hallucinating.

"Come thou sanctifier, almighty and eternal Master and bless this sacrifice prepared for the glory of thy holy name." The wolf priest raised his hand. "May this incense which thou hast blessed, ascend to thee and may thy mercy descend upon us.

"Raurí Mac Cathail, you are here to go on your final journey. You shall have everlasting life for you will live on in the heavenly host. Prepare yourself for this holy sacrifice."

The priest drew back his lips, exposing long sharp fangs.

"Don't touch me," Raurí yelled, backing away.

He looked around seeking a way out of this bizarre place.

"Raurí, dear boy, you are part of the new and eternal covenant. Can you not see we offer you eternal life? Come to me all you who labour and I shall make you free."

With a sudden bound the priest leapt forward, taking Raurí by surprise. His robes billowed out and the priest hovered in the air, his black vestments flapping and keeping him aloft, like some vast bird of prey. While Raurí was watching the flying priest his attention was distracted from the acolytes. Suddenly he felt a sharp pain in his calf and jerked back.

"Damn it to hell!"

Glancing down he saw the small creatures gathered around him sinking teeth into his legs. Raurí yelled again and kicked at them. Even though he knew this was a dream, the bites felt very real. Raurí hopped around trying to dislodge the things. Then everything went dark and he felt a great weight on his shoulders as the priest dropped on top of him.

"Raurí," a voice intoned in his ear, "this day thou shall be with us in paradise."

Raurí screamed as he felt the fangs bite into his neck. He fought wildly, punching and kicking in almost total darkness as the robes of the priest enveloped him.

"Get off me, you pervert."

Raurí sank to his knees, feeling his resistance weakening. He knew a moment of despair as the weight of the wolf priest drove him to the floor. But yet he kept fighting, punching at the solid body of the priest who seemed impervious to his blows.

• • •

In the little cottage the two females worked over Raurí's seemingly lifeless body. It had taken them a while to prepare for the operation they were about to perform.

"You know this might not work," Aishling said, as she hoisted herself up on the bed and stretched out beside Raurí.

Her grandmother had inserted a hollow needle into the youth's arm to which was attached a narrow tube.

"There is a real possibility he will die anyway if we don't attempt it," Ina answered. "You have already bitten him, so perhaps that is enough to prepare his body for a transfer of your blood. We don't know enough about the workings of the human body to be certain about any of this."

"Have you thought of what will happen if he dies? You will have a dead body in your house. If it is discovered you might be accused of his murder."

Ina gave the younger woman a weary smile.

"Disposing of a dead body will not be a problem. What do you think happens to those poor aborted babes of those distraught women who come to me for deliverance?"

Aishling gave her grandmother a quizzical look.

"What does happen to them?"

"The bogs of Ireland hide many such secrets."

Ina worked steadily, connecting the youngsters via needles in their arms and a flexible tube with a clip keeping it closed off.

"Are you ready? Once I release the stopper, I want you to open and close your fist to help increase the flow. At anytime if you want to stop just tell me. In fact if you don't want to do this we can stop right now."

Aishling yawned lazily.

"Just get on with it, Grandma."

Ina reached over and released the clip.

● ● ●

Raurí was sinking beneath the weight of his attackers. At first he had threshed about wildly kicking out and punching, but even as he fought he felt himself growing weaker and weaker. All the while the attack was going on, the bizarre wolf-priest chanted, sometimes in Latin, sometimes in Gaelic and sometimes in English.

"Eternal rest grant onto them, O lord, and let perpetual light shine upon them. *Dies irae, dies illa.* Shall the world in ashes lie? Oh how great shall be the fear when they see their bones exposed."

Raurí felt a particularly jagged pain in his arm. It was as if sharp teeth had bitten, right down to the bone.

"Aaaahhhh! Goddamn!"

The acute pain seemed to jolt Raurí out of the weariness that was threatening to overwhelm him. Even though Raurí was convinced he was living a dream it was too real for comfort. With this realization came the thought that what he was experiencing was more than a dream.

What if something or someone had killed him and he was now in Hades or purgatory or the world between the living and the dead? The thought frightened Raurí and in a panic he made fresh efforts to fight back. With a sudden renewal of strength he struggled to roll over. The ploy was successful and the wolf-priest let out a snarl of protest as Raurí ended up on top.

Raurí drove his fist into his attacker's ribs and the wolf priest's snarl changed to grunt. For a moment the hold on Raurí slackened enough for the youngster to break free. He clambered to his feet and found two of the priest's helpers clinging to his legs, biting with their sharp little teeth. Raurí limped to the side of the chapel dragging the creatures with him and slammed his leg against the wall. There was squeal and he lost one of the little biters. He repeated the same action and managed to dislodge the second acolyte from his other leg. But by this time the wolf-priest was on his feet and had resumed his chanting.

"Death and nature then shall quake as the dead from dust awake. *Ante diem rationis.*"

As he intoned the stanzas, the black garbed priest again rushed at Raurí. By now the youngster was recovering his strength. It was as if some new source of energy was flooding into his veins. There was that, and the fact that he was becoming angry. This time Raurí surprised his assailant by lowering his head and driving at the priest. The chanting was suddenly cut off as Raurí struck the priest solidly in the chest. Something gave under the impact and the priest fell away howling and cursing vilely.

"May your soul rot in hell. Get the blasphemer. Chop his legs from him."

The diminutive beasts jumped up and down, shrieking and showing their sharp little teeth. Raurí looked round for some escape from this nightmare. There was only one way to go and that was towards the rear of the chapel, so he ran. Behind him the priest screeched out orders and he could hear the scrabbling of claws on the stone floor as the beast things pursued him.

A door—a dark wooden door. Raurí hurled himself against it, his hands groping for a latch or handle. Something hit him on the back and he felt sharp teeth and claws dig into him.

"Damn it," he yelled, squirming about in agony.

He turned and slammed his back against the door hoping to squash the thing causing him so much pain. Raurí overbalanced as the door opened and he fell backwards, out into darkness.

CHAPTER FOUR

Ina closed the clip on the transfer tube connecting Aishling and Raurí.

"I think that should be enough for now. We have done what we can to help him. The rest is up to him. If he has strength and courage and fighting spirit he might survive."

She removed the tube from her granddaughter's arm and pressed a cotton pad against the puncture.

"How do you feel?"

Aishling sat up.

"Okay."

The girl stared past her grandmother. Ina whipped her head round to see what had drawn the girl's attention. Damian was peering around the door. The older woman relaxed as she saw him.

"I couldn't stay outside. I need to know how he is. Will he be all right?"

Damian's eyes were bloodshot and red-rimmed as if he had spent his time outside weeping.

"Your friend needs rest and warmth. It is too soon to know if we have been successful or not."

Ina turned and gazed down at the pale face of the unconscious youth.

"He would have died had you not brought him to us. Now we can only wait and watch over him. You can sit with him if you like."

Damian came inside and shuffled forward to the bed. He smiled wanly at Aishling as she rose from where she had been lying beside Raurí.

"Are you his betrothed?"

"You are a quaint creature. But Grandma is right. He wouldn't have survived without your help."

She stretched lazily and Damian was reminded of an animal awaking from sleep, tensing and relaxing limbs.

"Would you like something to eat?" Ina asked him. "We're about to carry on with our breakfast."

"Nothing for me. If it is all right I'll just sit here and watch over him."

Ina pulled a chair over beside the bed.

"Here, make yourself comfortable. If you notice any change, call me immediately."

Back in the kitchen Ina warmed over her porridge. Aishling disappeared into the small pantry and returned carrying a whole rabbit.

"I'm starving."

She sat the carcass on the table and skinned it, using a slender knife. Ina brought a jug and a beaker and set it beside the girl.

"Here's your water, you'll need to drink plenty."

Aishling expertly sliced into the neck of the rabbit then deftly tugged at the pelt exposing the flesh. The girl bit into the meat and chewed steadily. There was silence as the two women fed; the younger on the raw flesh of the rabbit and the older one on porridge and ribbons of bacon.

● ● ●

When Raurí fell on his back the thing clinging to him squealed once and went silent but more of the creatures were crowding through the doorway. Raurí scrambled to his feet even as they launched themselves at him. Wildly he punched and kicked, bowling one or two over. Then the bizarre wolf-priest appeared and howled into the night sky.

"If I'm dead then this must be hell," Raurí moaned.

Raurí drove a fist into the mouthful of teeth coming at him as the priest attacked. The priest's yelp of anguish momentarily stopped the onslaught of his beast helpers. Raurí remembered a piece of advice from his Uncle Ivor.

"When the odds are steep, the feet are fleet."

Raurí turned and fled into the night. Behind him he could hear the wolf priest howling. It sent prickles of fear up the naked youth's spine. To his consternation, the howl was answered from somewhere out in the night. The calls were long and mournful. They filled the night with an eerie sound not unlike the swirl of *uilleann* pipes that Raurí occasionally heard played at a *ceilidh* or at the occasional wake for the dead. He ran, and as he went he felt his strength and senses returning.

The scents and noises of the night swept over him. Sounds were magnified. He imagined he heard paws padding though the darkness. Somewhere wings fluttered as a bird—most likely an owl—swept out to hunt. Raurí imagined small furry creatures listening in trepidation as they watched for predators. He smelled pine needles and leaf mould as it was disturbed by running paws tracking him.

In a strange way this whole experience, though frightening, was also exhilarating; as if he was being tested for resilience and endurance. Raurí ran on, smelling the night air, sensing obstacles even as he came to them and swerving around trees and bushes and avoiding a collision. It was as if his senses were sharpened and he could hear and see things that otherwise he would have missed.

Now that he was free of the burial chapel he had a definite lifting of spirit. The howling continued and he had an urge to reply. As he ran he felt himself responding to the wildness he sensed around him. He felt his body stiffening and put it down to the injuries he had sustained in the fight in the chapel. And then his pace faltered for his limbs were jerking and shifting as if under forces he was unable to control. He stumbled and fell to the soil; the smell of vegetation and earth and night strong in his nostrils. His arms jerked and he felt as if his joints were being pulled apart. His legs thrashed and twitched as the same thing was happening to his lower limbs.

"Aaaahhhh!"

Raurí writhed in agony in the dirt, screaming out his anguish while his body shuddered and jerked and his bones shifted inside his skin. And his skin—it was an agony of itching as if swarms of ants were marching across his body.

"What the hell is happening to me?"

Raurí whimpered and cringed as his body went through its agony. All around him the howling persisted, making the night noisy with their eerie sounds. Suddenly Raurí lifted his face to the sky and hollered in reaction to the feral violence that he sensed all around him. His howls were also in response to the pain surging through him as his body contorted. As he bawled, the pain eased somewhat and Raurí clambered to his feet. He did not get far before he realized he was on all fours.

Raurí tried to stand and to his surprise bounded forward. He looked down and was somewhat puzzled by the strange paw-like things he could see at the end of his arms. Raurí shook himself and found he was quite stable on all fours. He took a tentative move forward. His legs responded awkwardly and he tumbled over and floundered on the ground.

He took more notice of his body and was disconcerted to find he was covered in fur—thick black fur that contrasted so starkly with the naked body he had started out with. Tentatively he stood once more and cautiously placed his arms ahead of him. He was somewhat fascinated as he observed his fur covered limbs.

Dammit, he had changed into a dog.

Raurí bounded forward. And this time remained upright. He increased the pace and remained stable. In great wonderment he found he was bounding along on all fours. Raurí threw himself into this new experience.

It seemed to him since the *ceilidh* his whole life had taken on a new and fantastic aspect. First the weird wolf-chapel and wolf creatures that attacked him and now he was having hallucinations that he had transformed into a wolf. Raurí ran on and behind him he heard the wolf-priest howling as he followed somewhere in the rear. Raurí raised his head and howled in response.

"Damn you, I am your equal now. Catch me if you can."

He had the feeling his voice was coming out different as if he too was barking in wolf tones. On he ran and from all around he heard wolf voices calling in response to his challenge.

His senses sharpened and the smells of the countryside were quick in his nostrils. He smelt trees and distinguished pine from oak and chestnut. The beating of tiny wings fluttered in his ears. Small feet padded through the trees or dug and scrabbled in the earth, all seeking the same thing. A hunger drove them on, for night was the time of the hunter, and predators were out prowling for food.

Food was a living morsel that walked or crawled or flew and had to be tracked down and cornered and killed and consumed. All around him he could sense this process going on. This was the way the earth progressed through cycles of life and death. Predator and prey. An eternal dance of death repeated ceaselessly since the beginning of time when other creatures of another age stalked their food and attacked swiftly and dealt out death so that they might themselves survive.

Raurí ran on with the smells of the night strong in his nostrils. He smelt the clouds and the trees and the earth and the creatures that crawled and crept and ran upon it. He was one of the swift ones. He could feel his strength and the fleetness of his limbs.

"Come and get me," he yelled. "I'm here"

The challenge went out and was answered by other voices of the night. He threw back his head and howled at the moon. Out of the darkness another form rose as if from the earth. Raurí skidded to a halt, his paws gouging tracks in the earth as he slowed and stopped.

"I am Raurí Mac Cathail," he snarled. "I am death."

"Raurí Mac Cathail, if you wish to live through this night then come stand by me. There are those following you who want to corrupt your blood. If they succeed they will trap you in their own world. They are the Wolfessa and are condemned to live and hunt in this underworld—neither living nor dead."

The strange wolf was blonde and strong and Raurí could smell the female musk coming off her.

"Why are you here?"

"I am here to help you survive. Trust me. Quickly, they are almost here."

Something about the timbre of the strange she-wolf's voice seemed familiar. Raurí paced forward and stood beside her.

"Do not be afraid," the she-wolf assured him. "When your enemies come it will be a fight to the death. Show no mercy for they will show none to you."

The newcomer had hardly finished speaking when there was a sudden rush of movement out of the darkness. The she-wolf leapt to meet the dark shadow charging out of the night. A ferocious snarling erupted as the two wolves met in midair; white teeth luminescent in the gloom.

The battling beasts fell to the earth and the snarling intensified. Raurí darted forward to help but before he could engage in the fight a dark shape hurtled out of the night crashing into him, sending him tumbling to earth. Before Raurí could get to his feet the wolf was on top of him, vicious fangs seeking his throat. Instinctively Raurí dropped his head and instead of closing on his throat the sharp fangs clashed against his lips and teeth.

Ignoring the pain, Raurí pushed his snout under his attacker's head and tried for a hold on the throat. His teeth closed on air as the other wolf leapt away. With a growl Raurí was on his feet facing his opponent. Behind him he could hear the struggle as the blonde wolf fought her own battle.

Attack is often the best method of defence; his Uncle Ivor had told him from time to time. Raurí immediately leapt forward. His opponent was bulky and very strong, as Raurí quickly discovered. Even as he attacked, the other wolf also leapt forward. Just in time Raurí twisted to one side and as he did so he slashed with bared teeth at the others exposed flank. He achieved nothing only a bruising pain on his already damaged snout.

The wolf turned swiftly and powerful jaws clamped on Raurí's spine. It was an agonizing grip and Raurí squealed as his hind legs went from under him. Those fangs bit deep and Raurí was powerless in their grip.

Frantically he struggled, his paws gauging bits of dirt and grass as he

A FEROCIOUS SNARLING ERUPTED AS THE TWO WOLVES MET IN MIDAIR...

tried to free himself from that debilitating grip. But there was no letup of the pressure on his hindquarters. In his struggles his paws encountered a stout stick and Raurí thought to use it as a weapon. It was then he discovered the limitations of a paw with talons, instead of a hand with fingers.

"Oh for a pair of hands," he howled in frustration.

He felt the change in his forelegs as they contracted and changed shape. There came a new agony as the fur on the limb retreated and bones shifted and ached and pale skin emerged along his arm once more.

"Aaaahhhh."

The pain in his spine was unremitting and agonizing. The stick was in his hand now and he twisted around with his upper body changing but neither wolf nor man as Raurí left off wanting the human form. The stick was jagged and broken at one end and Raurí rammed it into the eye socket of his opponent.

The stricken wolf convulsed and the pressure on Raurí's spine eased. Raurí pushed the stick deeper into the eye socket twisting it as he did so. His opponent let go its paralyzing hold and fell away howling. For a moment it stood there shaking its head and crying in pain and frustration. Raurí lunged again with the stick, aiming for the uninjured eye. The wolf tried to dodge but the end of the stick grazed the eyeball. Swiftly it turned and bounded away. It did not see the tree in its way and crashed headlong into the solid trunk of an oak. Raurí felt himself changing back to wolf form. Black hair raced along his forearm and his hands became hairy paws with talons.

Quickly he leapt forward. The distressed wolf was going round in circles moaning piteously. Raurí's fangs closed on his opponent's throat. He could feel the teeth going in, biting through fur and skin and he growled low in his throat and shook his head from side to side as he tried to do as much damage as possible.

A terrible howling echoed in his ear and the blinded wolf struggled to free itself from that deadly grip. But Raurí was not to be shaken off, his teeth deep in the wolf's throat. The tang and smell of blood incensed him and he growled and bit harder and shook his head from side to side, the other wolf helpless in his grip.

Deeper he bit, his fangs doing terrible damage. The wolf was convulsing as it struggled vainly to extricate itself from the death grip. Without warning its legs gave way and it fell sideways with Raurí on top, still holding and biting and growling.

Blood was running on his chest and the smell strong in his nostrils, seemingly more potent with his wolf's sense of smell. Desperate panting noises were coming from the throat of the wounded wolf as its windpipe was crushed. Its legs trashed about and talons gouged clumps from the forest floor. Weaker and weaker became its struggles. Deeper and deeper sank Rauri's fangs until his victim grew still and struggled no more.

Rauri held his grip shaking his head from side to side as he attempted to do more damage but there was no reaction from the stricken wolf. Cautiously, he released his grip. The wolf sank lifelessly to the dirt. Rauri stood back watching carefully in case his victim suddenly leapt back to life again. It lay motionless, its throat a ruined, bloody mess. Rauri raised his snout to the moon and howled. It was an exultant cry of victory. He had fought and conquered his enemy.

"I am Rauri Mac Cathail," he howled, "invincible killer."

His call echoed through the trees. Another voice joined him and he turned in surprise. The blonde wolf stood nearby, her head held high as she howled out her own victory chant. Rauri could see dark stains of blood around her muzzle. Abruptly she ceased her howling.

"Come," she growled, "We must get to a place of safety."

She turned and bounded into the forest. Rauri followed. They fled though the night and above them the stars glittered and a hunter's moon beamed down. A newly blooded male wolf and a mysterious female glided through the trees and the denizens of the forest stilled their movements and watched in trepidation until the pair had passed.

CHAPTER FIVE

Damian Hughes shivered and prayed and wept in turn as he watched over Rauri. The youth called out in his sleep, twisted and turned in the bed, and at one stage sat up, his eyes open wide. Rauri's mouth also opened and Damian's blood ran cold as he heard the terrible howling and saw the expression in Rauri's eyes.

"Oh dear God, what is happening to my poor boy?"

Ina came in the room when she heard the noise. She came over and took Rauri's hand in hers. The youngster was shaking, his limbs vibrating at an astonishing rate.

"Can't we do anything for him?" Damian pleaded.

"His pulse is very fast and yet he is so cold."

Even as she spoke Raurí's limbs jerked more violently so he was in danger of falling off the bed.

"Hold him while I get more blankets."

Damian's strong arms wrapped round the youth and he held him tightly.

"Don't worry Raurí, I'm here," he whispered. "I'll look after you just like you looked after me."

Raurí struggled against his friend's grasp. His mouth opened and he ground his teeth. Spittle dribbled on his chin and he snarled like an animal. It was as well Damian was so strong for Raurí thrashed and struggled violently in his embrace.

"Raurí, Raurí, don't take on so. It's me, your friend, Damian. I won't let anything happen to you. Not to you Raurí, my poor precious boy."

Tears were streaming down Damian's cheeks as he strove to keep Raurí in the bed. Ina returned with blankets and together they draped them around the agitated youth. While they worked, Raurí snarled and bit the air as if fighting some invisible enemy. Eventually they succeeded in wrapping the blankets tightly around him. It was easier for Damian to keep Raurí's struggles under control now he was enveloped within the covers. Ina looked shrewdly at the hunchback.

"You look exhausted. Go and get some rest. I'll look after him for now."

"No, he is my friend and I'll stay. What is happening to him?"

"Raurí is fighting on another level. There are forces trying to destroy him. There is no guarantee he will survive. We can only hope he has the courage and the will to endure whatever trials he is going through. All we can do is keep him safe in this world and make sure he does not harm himself. The next twenty-four hours will be crucial. If he survives that long then he has every chance of coming through. I can tell you now: others have undergone the same process and not lived to tell the tale. It takes a special courage and ability to survive this."

Damian was staring at healer.

"What are you telling me or not telling me?"

Ina glanced sharply at Damian.

"Perhaps I have said too much."

She turned to leave. Damian's hand snaked out and grasped her arm.

"Tell me what is going on?" he demanded.

Ina looked pointedly at Damian's hand on her arm but Damian did not take the hint.

"Tell me what is happening. I need to know. He is my friend."

Damian glanced down at Raurí who seemed to have quietened for the moment.

"He is the only one who treated me as an equal. Every man's hand was against me. I was friendless and an outcast. People threw stones at me and made the sign of the evil eye when they caught sight of me. Raurí Mac Cathail gave me self-respect and something more precious. He gave me his friendship. If need be I would lay down my life for him. If you tell me now that would help him I would do it."

Ina sighed deeply and reached out to prise Damian's fingers from her arm. She moved past him and sat on the edge of the bed.

"If you love Raurí as you say you do, and I have no reason to doubt you, then you must never breathe a word of what I am about to tell you."

Damian nodded.

"It has always been known man is but a higher breed of animal. Often the being we call human got a bit mixed up and a creature that was neither animal nor human emerged. Such aberrations were believed to be caused by evil forces and were destroyed soon after they were born. Some, however, survived. But in order to survive, these divergent creatures had to blend into the dangerous world of the humans and disguise their true dual nature. And so they developed the ability to take on human shape when necessary, and only become their animal self when safe to do so."

"What has this to do with Raurí being beaten half to death?"

Damian asked staring down at the restless Raurí as he strained against the constraints of the blankets wrapped tightly around his body.

"Are you trying to tell me the men who did this are animals?"

"Patience, my man—patience—all will be revealed. What I am telling you is that we are all animals only some of us are more animal than others. When you brought Raurí to me he was all but dead. There was little chance he would survive. I have a friend who is akin to the type of person I am trying to tell you about. She has the ability to change from human to animal."

"What the hell are you saying?"

"Will you listen? Such a person can change from human to animal and retain all the strengths and abilities of both species, thereby enhancing their capability to survive even such serious injuries as has happened to your friend. There was a slim chance of survival for Raurí only if we were to transfer blood from my changeling acquaintance to Raurí. I hoped he would take on the animal form and be better equipped to fight the death that was about to overwhelm him."

Ina thought it best not to mention that Raurí might have been infected previously when Aishling bit him during their lovemaking.

"Raurí is warring with forces that would destroy him. You are witnessing that struggle now as Raurí fights for survival. While his body jerks and moans and thrashes about in that bed, his spirit is fighting on another plane. I have sent someone to help him. We can only watch over him and make sure he is safe while he battles to survive."

Damian was shaking his head.

"Look I'm grateful to you for trying to help Raurí but this mumbo jumbo, animal stuff is nonsense. I know that's how you make a living, selling spells and potions to poor ignorant craters that come here for help. But it doesn't cut it with me. As long as you help Raurí, that's all that matters to me."

At that moment Raurí opened his eyes, stared around him, moaned, then closed his eyes again and was still. Ina reached out and felt for his pulse.

CHAPTER SIX

When Raurí awoke the first thing he saw was the anxious face of Damian. Seeing his friend was reassuring after the strange nightmare he had been living. Raurí was just glad to be awake and didn't care where he was as long as he had escaped the frightening wolf dream. Pain swamped his body as awareness flooded back. A bass drum was slowly pounding his brain to porridge. His face felt stiff and sore, his teeth ached and every bone in his body had its own core of agony.

"I feel like hell," he groaned, afraid to move in case the hurt increased.

"Raurí, thank God you're awake. How do you feel?"

"Where the hell am I?"

"Ina Riley's place. I'd better call her and tell her you're awake."

"Wait, what the hell am I doing here? Or is this still part of my nightmare?"

"It's no dream, Raurí. I brought you here for you were bad hurt. I didn't know what else to do."

Raurí stared up at the concerned face of his friend.

"What are you talking about?"

"Don't you remember what happened to you?"

"I remember the *ceilidh*. I met a girl—she was very special." Suddenly Raurí's eyes widened. "You say this is Ina Riley's place. Did Aishling bring me back here? I can't remember that part of it. Jeez, it must have been some night. Every bone in my body is aching. What did she do to me? I feel as if I've been pushed through a turnip chopper." Raurí glanced around the room as if to make sure they were alone. "Aishling," he said in a low voice, "old Ina Riley's granddaughter. I met her at the *ceilidh*. I remember being with her but nothing much after that. And now I wake up in her house. What the heck is going on? You don't think the tales about Ina are true and she is some sort of witch? I never believed such superstitions myself but can you explain how it is I wake up in Ina Riley's house and don't remember how I got here?"

"Raurí, it was me brought you here. I found you lying in a gully half-dead. I carried you here for I couldn't think of where else to bring you. I thought for sure you were dead."

Raurí stared at Damian trying to make sense of what he had said.

"What are you talking about? How come I was lying in a ditch?"

And Damian decided not to tell Raurí who it was that had attacked him.

"Raurí, I don't know. I knew you were at the *ceilidh* and I was hoping to meet up with you for a bit of *craic*. I found you laying there, more dead than alive. I brought you here. I'd better tell Ina you're awake."

Before Damian could move the door opened and Ina stuck her head around the door.

"I heard voices. Has your man come too?"

Raurí felt apprehensive as he watched the healer come into the room. He wasn't sure if she knew about him and Aishling. She came to the bed and placed her hand on his forehead.

"Mmm... still a bit feverish." She took his wrist to assess his pulse. "Seems a trifle thready. How do you feel?"

"I feel like a herd of cattle have trampled me and then came back for another go. Thank you for your hospitality. I'd best be getting back home now."

Raurí eased back the covers in order to sit up. To his consternation he found his legs wouldn't obey him. He felt weak as a newborn puppy and his head was spinning. He might have toppled out of bed only Damian's strong arm grabbed him.

"I don't think you'll be going anywhere, young man. You're far too weak. You need rest and good food. Has Damian told you, you might have died if he hadn't found you?"

Raurí lay in the bed exhausted by his brief attempt to move. His entire body was a drumbeat of agony.

"I feel like I'm dying now. What happened to me?"

"Didn't Damian tell you?"

"He said he found me in a ditch. I know I was drinking but it wasn't enough to make me fall down."

"We can only assume someone had it in for you and beat you up. There are bruises and cuts all over your body. Whoever it was intended to kill you. Can you think of anyone that might have it in for you?"

Raurí frowned as he thought of people who might want to give him a good kicking.

"I can't think of anyone. I ain't got an enemy in the world."

"Well whatever, you're lucky to be alive. You have Damian here to thank for that."

Raurí stared up at his friend. Damian turned away a flush creeping up his normally pallid face.

"You're a goddamn hero, Damian. When I get out of this bed, you and I are going out on a spree and we'll get so drunk we'll need a week to get over it."

Damian didn't know where to look. Raurí's offer made him happy and sad at the same time. No one had ever offered to take him anywhere. He said nothing and stared at the floor. Another head poked inside the room, this time crowned with a halo of golden hair.

"How's the patient?"

Raurí stared at Aishling. At that moment, weak and vulnerable as he was, he could feel a stirring in his loins.

"I'm all right," he said lamely. "I'm trying to figure out what happened to me. I remember the *ceilidh,* but nothing after that. Damian says he found me half dead and brought me here. Someone must have jumped me and gave me a good hammering. Did you enjoy the dance?" he asked, not daring to look in Ina's direction.

"Very much." She frowned. "You didn't upset anyone at the *ceilidh* did you; have arguments or a fight or something?"

"Not that I recall. I did meet a very attractive young woman."

He grinned impishly, watching her reaction.

"What else do you remember?"

"The dance—meeting you—that's all; I don't even remember leaving the *ceilidh.*"

"Nothing else? What about when you were unconscious? Or is it just a blank until you woke up here?"

"There was a dream," Raurí said slowly, "a horrible dream—more a nightmare than a dream."

"A nightmare?"

Aishling came and perched on the edge of the bed.

"What kind of nightmare?"

He felt a strong attraction to the young woman and even as he lay in bed, weak and debilitated and aching to the very core of his body, he longed for her to slip under the covers with him. Only for the fact Damian and Ina being present he might have attempted to entice her to indulge him.

"Tell me about the nightmare," she insisted.

"Wolves," he said thoughtfully, "there were wolves in the dream." He shook his head in wonderment. "Why should I be dreaming about wolves?"

"What kind of wolves?"

"That was the strangest thing. The wolves were in a chapel dressed up in the vestments like priests. They were praying and singing hymns and had a crucible with incense, only the fragrance was more earthy than scented. It was like a funeral service with me the dead person. I managed to escape. Then the most bizarre thing happened. As I fled it was as if I was transformed into a wolf also. I ran into the forest and I was joined by another wolf and we fought other wolves. It was all so real."

"It does seem all rather connected," observed Ina. "Dreams have a weird way of telling us things about ourselves that are otherwise hidden from us. Perhaps all will be revealed in the fullness of time. Anyway, that's enough talking for now. I'll bring you a bite to eat and then you'd better get some rest. You have some way to go to regain your health."

Ina got up and left the room.

"Maybe I should be going," Damian ventured.

Raurí paid no heed to him, all his attention on Aishling sitting on his bed, so tantalizingly near. When there was no response after voicing his intention to leave, Damian shuffled awkwardly to the door. He looked regretfully at his friend then went out and quietly closed the door behind him.

Raurí stared into Aishling's intense yellow eyes and for a moment, was remembering the dream. He was living again that animal coupling he had experienced in a forest glade beneath a full moon. There came a knock on the door and Ina pushed into the room carrying a tray of food. She smiled at Raurí.

"There's a bit of colour in your cheeks, Raurí. We must be doing something right"

CHAPTER SEVEN

R\aurí slept late the next morning. When he awoke the drapes on the window were still in place. The room was dark but even so he sensed someone in the room.

"Is that you, Aishling?" he whispered, as he spied the dark figure sitting nearby.

"No it's not Aishling, you buck eejit," a familiar voice answered. "What the goddamn hell have you been up to? I had to leave everything and come over here to see to you. I left that damned familiar of yours in charge. I only hope he doesn't wreck the place before I get back."

"Uncle Ivor! "

Ivor drew back the curtains. Light flooded the room and Raurí flinched as the brightness hit his eyes. His uncle dragged the chair over to the bed and sat. Critically he examined Raurí.

"They made a fine mess of your face. Tell me what happened."

Raurí told him what little he knew.

"So the outcast found you. He didn't tell me that part of it. Just said as how you had been hurt and Ina Riley had taken you in. Why couldn't he have told me it was him as rescued you. He's a strange misbegotten creature."

"According to Ina I was near death when Damian brought me here. It's a sobering thought that you owe your life to someone. How do you ever repay a debt like that?"

"You don't. During my time fighting the Boers I learned that. You have formed a bond with that pariah that can only be broken by death."

"Uncle Ivor, stop calling him pariah," Raurí said testily. "Call him Damian or Hughes but not outcast or pariah."

"Okay, okay. What's in a name anyway? I was called all sorts of things when I was in the British Army. Bog-trotter, Turf-arse, Paddy Fuckwit, Paddy Shite-for-brains, Seamus the sheep-shagger. I've forgotten half the things that were thrown at me. You learn to pay no attention after a while. At first I would thump the fella as called me. But that only got me pack-drill for fighting. I hit an officer once who told me I was fathered on an Irish cow by my parish priest. I didn't mind the priest bit but I couldn't let the insult to Irish cows go unchallenged. I got thirty lashes for that outburst. After that I learned to keep my fists in my pockets."

Raurí grinned back at his uncle.

"I never know when you are making up these stories or when you are telling the truth of it."

"Now isn't that the mark of a true bard. Anyway, who was it did this to you?"

"I don't know. I can remember the *ceilidh*. I remember dancing with the girls and drinking Sean Murphy's poteen; but nothing beyond that. Next thing I know I wake up here with Damian watching over me."

"You weren't meant to survive this. From what Ina tells me she didn't think you would live beyond the next morning. Someone has it in for you. Can you make a guess who it might be wants you dead?"

"Uncle Ivor, I can't think of a soul that would want to kill me. Maybe a madman escaped from the asylum and roaming loose."

"Humph, there's been no report of any such escape. If such a thing happened you can be sure it would be all over the papers. It's a real mystery. When you leave this sickbed you'll have to be on your guard at all times. If someone went to this bother to murder you there's a possibility he'll try again." Ivor shook his head. "If only you could remember. Maybe it will come to you eventually. If we know who we're dealing with then we can take steps to prevent it happening again." He stood up. "I can see you're in good hands here. I asked Ina about paying her for looking after you but she wouldn't hear tell of it. I brought her some victuals but it is poor enough repayment for what she is doing."

"I'm sorry to put you to all this bother."

"And so you should be, you bloody fool."

Ivor reached out and patted Raurí's shoulder. The youngster winced as his uncle's callused hand stirred up pain in his damaged body.

"Still tender I see. Well, I'd better be getting back. I'll try and come again. Is there anything you need that I can bring you?"

"I can't think of anything. How will you manage without me there to help out?"

"Well, I suppose I could ask your friend, Damian, if he'd like to stay on until you're fit again."

Raurí grinned up at his uncle feeling the stiffness in his face as he did so.

"Don't be too hard on the old booger. Tell him he's taking my place and doing me a favour by doing so. That should please him."

His uncle was shaking his head.

"You and Damian—what an unlikely pairing. Prince Charming and his familiar."

Before Raurí could reprove him for such an unfair comparison, his uncle left the room. Raurí relaxed back in the bed and contemplated his situation. Before long the door opened again and Aishling and Ina came in; the younger woman carrying a tray.

"Good morning," Ina greeted him, "how is the patient this morning?"

Raurí was staring at Aishling and for a moment did not answer. She looked so beautiful his heart constricted in his chest. There was something otherworldly about the young woman, as if she had so much vitality it was like a physical force coming off her. Even her hair, which made Raurí think of spun gold, seemed to glow as if some inner light was shining through. Ina examined him holding his wrist to measure his pulse and placing her hand on his brow.

"The fever seems to have abated and your pulse is much stronger. In a day or two we'll have you back at your uncle's creamery churning out butter and cheese by the bucket load."

"Here's your breakfast," Aishling said. "I hope you're hungry."

"I sure am. I could eat the hind leg of a donkey."

"Can you sit up?"

"Sure."

Raurí winced as he tried to do as she asked. He was still very stiff and sore. Aishling sat the tray before him. Her closeness was making him lightheaded. He could smell her animal-like musky tang and once more he was reminded of his hallucinations in the forest of wolves when he had frolicked with a golden-furred, young she-wolf. Quickly he tried to blot out the images and concentrated on Aishling's eyes. They glowed with an almost hypnotic intensity.

Golden eyes, he thought, and golden hair.

"Do you want me to feed you?"

He did, but didn't think it was proper to be fed like an invalid.

"Thanks but I can handle it."

He managed to tear his eyes from Aishling and looked down at the tray. His mouth watered at the sight of the heaped dish of bacon, eggs and liver along with a steaming mug of tea. He had never been fond of liver but his mouth salivated at the sight of that blood-engorged organ.

"I never realized how hungry I was."

He grabbed up the knife and fork and became immediately engrossed in the food. Never had food tasted so succulent. Every mouthful was a wonder of seasoning and smell. It was as if his taste buds had been enhanced so as to tease out the flavour of every morsel.

"I'll bring you some bread."

"Yeah, please."

He nodded his head while busily chewing; the heap of food disappearing rapidly. When Aishling returned with a plate of fresh bread and a bowl of butter, he had finished the cooked food. Raurí spread butter on the bread and chewed contentedly washing it down with hot tea.

"I'd better bring you more tea."

"This is butter made at Uncle Ivor's creamery."

"Yes, when he came last night he brought a hamper of produce for us. It's as well he did at the rate you're consuming it."

Raurí suddenly stopped eating.

"I... I'm sorry. I never thought. Will you have enough for yourselves?"

The women were amused by his obvious embarrassment.

"Oh, Raurí, just eat up. It's good to see a young fella with a healthy appetite. It means you are mending. Your uncle promised to bring more. You need to eat well to heal that busted body of yours. As long as you are here under our care we'll just keep feeding you up."

"I guess I'll never be able to repay you for all you done for me."

"You'll repay us by getting well. Once we have you up and about again there are plenty of things you can do for us. We need turf cutting. The roof needs mending. It's shedding thatch every high wind we get. Rain is leaking into some of the rooms. The pump in the yard is getting a bit worn. You'll be here for years working off your debt."

Raurí was not to know Ina Riley was teasing him, but the prospect of spending his time at the cottage with Aishling for company sounded a pleasant way of working off his debt.

"Right, let's get these dishes cleared up. It's market day in Rosslea and that's where I'm headed as soon as I have cleared up. Is there anything you want when I'm there?"

The women left Raurí contentedly lying back on his pillows. He could hear them chattering as they made out a shopping list. Their voices faded as he gradually dozed off.

The dream was so vivid he moaned out loud. Aishling was in bed with him and her hand was stroking him.

"I love you Aishling. Will you marry me?"

She stuck her tongue in his ear.

"Don't be stupid. Why would I want to marry a bosthoom like you?"

The dream was so real he didn't want it to end but found himself drifting towards wakefulness.

"You're the most exciting woman I have ever met."

Then her lips were pressed against his and he felt her tongue caressing his lips. He opened his eyes and she was there beside him. The fog of sleep lifted as he realized this was no dream.

"Aishling," he croaked.

His hands reached for her and she was naked beneath the blankets. He felt her leg glide across him. Her lips never left his and her tongue was inside his mouth. She slid on top of him her smooth skin gliding over him like silk over glass.

He felt the intensity of his desires grow as she moved on top of him. He felt her respond as she mewed into his face. For ecstatic moments their world was all sound and fury.

Raurí recovered well enough to leave his sickbed and join the women for meals. He experienced mild light-headedness and his body was stiff and sore but otherwise he was in pretty good shape for someone who had been at death's door.

Every night Aishling came to his bed and the youngsters made love into the late hours. Because of Raurí's weakened condition Aishling took the dominant position, mewling and growling like a young rutting animal. Disconcerting though it was initially, Raurí came to accept his lover's abandoned behaviour. In fact it unleashed something of the beast in him and he found himself biting at Aishling's naked breasts, drawing cries of pain and pleasure from her. At times Raurí wondered what Ina must have made of their behaviour for they were wondrously noisy.

The trio lived in a small thatched cottage and noises in one room could easily be heard in another. But the healer seemed oblivious to the sexual activities going on under her roof, or else she chose to ignore it, for when she came to minister to him or check his condition she made no reference to their nightly antics.

"I think fresh air would do you a power of good," Aishling announced one afternoon.

"Yeah, that would be good. I never did like being housebound."

As he stepped from the cottage, Raurí stood for a moment, gazing out towards the low hills in the distance. Before him the flat stippled green fields stretched out towards a row of trees that glowered in a surly smudge against the pale blue sky, studded with thick woolly clouds. A slight breeze had sprung up and gently shook small trees and bushes so the land seemed alive and breathing.

He could smell the dull odour of cut turf stacked in a corner beneath a roughly thatched shelter. The cover smelt musty and old and moved slightly in the breeze as if small creatures crept around inside. And indeed he felt he could sense tiny rodents snuffling in alarm as the humans stepped outside.

From far off he heard cattle lowing. The quick movement of birds caught his eye and he found himself following their swift movement as they flitted from bush to tree or soared into the air. Everything around him was alive and brimming with life and he could sense the spirit of the land as he had never experienced before. Raurí put his new awareness down to the fact that he had very nearly died and now he was sensing the gift of life that had been almost taken from him.

He ambled beside Aishling who seemed preoccupied as they walked. Raurí tried to make conversation but she answered only in monosyllables and seemed disinclined to talk. He wondered if something he had said or done had upset her but nothing came to mind. And then he began to fret that she was beginning to regret becoming involved with him. But hoped that might be unlikely as he was sure she enjoyed their lovemaking as much as he did. In the end he trailed off into silence.

As they walked there was a slight unsteadiness in his legs and he knew he was still weak. He was some way from being fully recovered and realized it would take time before he regained his full health.

They were climbing an incline towards a small conical hill with a crown of trees. Raurí frowned and slowed his steps as he stared up at the hill. He knew it for what it was. Locals believed these circular atolls were haunted by the little people.

"You're not superstitious?" Aishling asked, glancing sideways at him.

"No. Why are you asking?"

"I'm asking because we're heading up to those trees."

"Well, I'm not superstitious. And why are we going up there?"

"There's something I want to show you and we'll be less likely to be disturbed up there. People avoid such places because of superstitions attached tot them."

"Yeah, everyone believes the little people live there and it's bad luck to interfere with them."

"Do you believe that?"

"Nah, but I know people who swear they see lights at night and hear fairy music. Very few people have the courage to investigate."

"Well that will work to our advantage for what we have to do. We don't want to be disturbed."

"What have we to do anyway? This is all very mysterious." Raurí stopped, struck by a sudden thought. "You want to shag me out in the fresh air, is that it? You can't wait until tonight."

Aishling slipped her hand into his.

"Dear Raurí, there's more to life than shagging. No, this is something I have to show you. It is something we can't do back at the house. So we have come here for privacy."

Raurí was consumed with curiosity.

"This is all very mysterious. Can't you tell me?"

She squeezed his hand.

"Wait and see."

They walked hand in hand and for Raurí it was a peaceful and happy occasion; one that he was to look back upon and think that was his last moment of innocence, for nothing was to be the same after that day.

CHAPTER EIGHT

"Do you know anything about this place?" Aishling asked as they neared the top of the fairy hill. "Usually there are stories attached."

"Yes, it's called the Hill of Gaming.

"The Hill of Gaming; is that as in playing games or what?"

"No, it's about an addicted gambler called Emanon Fitzsimons. He would bet on anything and everything. Dog fighting, hare coursing, dog racing, cock fighting, horse racing, hurly games, boxing, wherever there were sporting events there was Fitzsimons placing bets. Anyway, some of his friends bet him he couldn't spend a night alone on this fairy hill. Fitzsimons took the bet and at dusk walked up the hill with a lamp and a blanket. Next morning his friends waited for the gambler to appear and when he did they were shocked at the change in him. When Fitzsimons walked down from the fairy hill his hair had turned white during the night. Fitzsimons never spoke of what happened during his vigil but from that day he never gambled again."

As Raurí finished his tale they arrived at the fringe of trees encircling the mound. The pair were silent as they threaded their way through the wooded perimeter. Twigs and leaves crunched underfoot as they progressed and then they were inside.

There was an air of solemnity associated with the space, probably induced by the feeling of entering a place cut off from the outside world.

FITZSIMONS WALKED UP THE HILL WITH A LAMP AND A BLANKET.

Aishling gazed around her for a few moments before turning back to her companion.

"Raurí, I am going to show you something. It might startle you at first but believe me there is nothing to be worried about."

She paused and gazed intently at him. Raurí gazed back into those deep yellow eyes; eyes that had the power to bewitch him so that he could not look into them without becoming aroused. He smiled at her, intrigued by her solemnity.

"You're going to call up the little people and put a spell on me," he joked. "You'll get them to make me your slave and do your every bidding. Yeah, I might be willing to go along with that."

"Raurí stay where you are for now and give me a little space." Aishling stepped back from him. "Whatever happens, just remember you are in no danger."

More intrigued than ever, Raurí smiled and nodded. Aishling had been wearing an embroidered shawl with a brass clasp at the neck in the shape of an animal paw. She reached up and undid the fastening and shrugged the garment from her shoulders. Underneath she was wearing a long cotton dress, turquoise in colour. Quickly she wriggled out of this and Raurí sucked in his breath as she stood naked before him.

Aishling had the full voluptuous body of a Greek goddess. The slight chill in the air had brought her nipples erect, their redness startling against the paleness of her skin. Raurí stared mesmerised as she stood before him, her golden mane matched by the flaxen hair nestling beneath her gently rounded belly.

"Aphrodite," Raurí breathed entranced by the blonde vision.

Instantly aroused, he involuntarily took a step forward but her upraised hand stopped him.

"Raurí please, just give me some space."

Reluctantly he held back and as he watched his arousal grew.

"Don't keep me waiting too long," he begged huskily. "There's only so much teasing a man can take."

She stretched, putting her arms above her head. Rising on her toes she interlaced her fingers and tensed. Raurí realized as he gazed on Aishling she was not just supremely feminine with all the curves of a desirable female but beneath that seductive shape she was also finely muscled. Bands of muscle writhed on her arms and legs and shoulders. She was swaying and moving her body in a way that emphasized this dynamic robustness. As Raurí stared in deepest admiration it was as if the muscles were expanding and writhing like independent organisms under that fair skin. And then illusion took over his senses for the muscular shapes were taking over her limbs and a furred haziness was growing upon her creamy skin.

"What the heck!"

The delusion heightened and it seemed as if that lovely form was gradually being covered in hair. On top of that, the female body shape was changing. Raurí stepped back as the illusory effects continued.

Aishling's face elongated and the forehead retreated. Teeth—no not teeth but fangs—yes, fangs! The hands warped and deformed into paws and then the illusion was complete as this Aishling being, that was not Aishling, dropped to all fours and a large ivory-coloured wolf stood in the fairy ring and gazed back at Raurí with those familiar yellow eyes. Raurí stumbled back, his hand to his mouth as he tried to shake off the phantasmagoria of the beast that stood in the place, where moments before, Aishling stood.

"What the hell! How did you do that?"

Raurí blinked his eyes, screwed them shut and opened them but the fantastical illusion remained.

"Aishling, what the hell's going on? Stop doing whatever you are doing. You drugged me, didn't you; you and that bloody witch grandmother of yours."

And then Raurí knew he was going mad for he recognized the wolf. He had met it in the nightmare he had endured before awakening in Ina Riley's house.

The wolf remained standing before Raurí, watching him with those strange golden eyes, so akin to Aishling's yellow eyes. It opened its mouth and barked. Raurí reversed further from the sprite that had taken Aishling's place, until he backed up against a tree. He reached behind him and the rough texture of the tree trunk slightly reassured him that some part of him he was still functioning normally.

The strange wolf thing continued yapping, staring earnestly at Raurí, as if trying to convey something to him. And a peculiar thing happened. Words seemed to be mingled with the barks.

Raurí stared at the wolf and the more he looked into those golden eyes the more he imagined the wolf was trying to talk to him. In spite of his fright he concentrated, thinking there might be some clue as to what was happening to him up here in this fairy ring. He remembered the tale of the gambler and his hair turning white and imagined his own hair was changing and he would wake up from this nightmare and find himself a white-haired old man.

"Woof-woof, Raurí, this is—woof what I am—woof."

The words becoming more distinct. Raurí concentrated. There was some clue in the strange almost human sounds coming from the throat of this transformed beast that once had the shape of a young woman.

"Listen, to me, Raurí."

The barking continued and more and more he was hearing the sound as a spoken language.

"This is what I am, and this is what you have become. We did it to save you. When Damian brought you to us you were as good as dead. The only way we could make sure of your survival was to give you a blood crossover."

"You've gave me something in my food? Stop it now. I don't like this joke. It's gone far enough!"

Raurí passed his hand in front of his eyes as if he could wipe away the disturbing apparition of a wolf that talked and that looked at him with Aishling's eyes. But when he looked again the phantom remained. Slowly the wolf sank to its haunches.

"Raurí, you must listen. It is for your own survival. You can't go back to your old life without knowing what has happened to you. Have you heard the term werewolf?"

Raurí knuckled his eyes and when he opened them again the only thing that had changed was hazy specks floating in his vision and then that cleared and the wolf illusion was still there.

"Raurí please listen. When you were lying injured, you were in a coma. Can you remember the dreams you were having? You said you were chased by wolves? A wolf came and fought side by side with you."

Raurí stared at the apparition.

"Yes, I told you all that."

"You didn't have to tell me about it. I was there. I was that wolf. You were fighting for your life. I came to help you. We fought the Wolfessa and then we made love as wolves and not as humans."

"How do you know that bit? I never told anyone that part. Wait a minute. I was talking in my sleep. You bloody listened and decided to play this trick on me. Well it's a lousy trick and I'm tired of it. I'm going back to the house and sleep off whatever it was you gave me."

"Raurí, don't you move. You're going to hear me out. I brought you out here to show you what you are; what you have become. You are one of us now. The dream of wolves you had was no dream. It was your wolf-spirit fighting for its life. If you had been overcome that night you would have become like the creatures that attacked you. A rogue animal that attacks humans and steals their souls so that imprisoned in a wolf body they can never return to human form. It is an aberration and abomination. They hunt for vulnerable humans. And they hunger for human flesh. That night as you lay near to death they were waiting for you on the other side. Ina transferred my blood to you. Without it you would have died. That is what kept you alive and gave you the strength to fight the Wolfessa."

Raurí was staring up into the sky, refusing to look at the make-believe wolf.

"Try it Raurí. Wish the change. Think yourself into a wolf's body."

"Stop it! I've had enough!"

He sensed movement and when he looked down the wolf had moved closer.

"Raurí, just for a moment pretend you believe what I'm telling you. Just pretend. Stare at your hand and wish the change. You don't have to go all the way. Just begin the change and then stop."

For long moments man and wolf stared at each other, the one with pleading in her eyes and the other with anguish. Slowly Raurí brought up his hand and stared at it. He frowned as he examined his hand and arm. For some reason he had never noticed how much hair grew upon his wrist and even upon the backs of his fingers. Was it always thus? On impulse he pulled open his shirt and stared at the matted hair upon his chest.

"No," he whispered.

"Do it, Raurí." The yellow eyes stared up at him, challenging. "What have you to lose?"

With an effort he broke eye contact and returned his attention to his hands; curled and uncurled them. Looking anew at the black hairs that sprouted upon his fingers; trying to imagine them as paws—paws of an animal—paws of a wolf; and felt a tremor go through him. Fascinated he stared and dared to imagine the transition from man to wolf.

Apprehension grew within him as he saw the knuckles flatten and the bones move beneath the skin and with the adjustment a throbbing similar to the ache from a day's labouring cutting turf that came from the constant grip on the shaft of the spade.

The ache was in his fingers and in his wrists and suddenly he was reminded of the fight in the dream world when he had fought the wolf and changed his paw to a hand in order to grasp a stick and use it as a weapon. The discomfort grew in his fingers and he saw them shorten and more hair erupted.

The pain in his nails intensified as he watched them thicken and grow and become sturdy claws. He stretched his arm out in front of him and stared at this strange limb that was attached to him but that could not be a part of him. His shoulders contracted and he felt the joints loosen and adjust as the change took over. And he screamed—more a howl of anguish and shook himself like a dog would do after awaking from sleep.

He cried out like a soul in torment but it sounded more like an animal yowling. He turned and smashed his hand—this animal hand that could be no part of him—against the tree. There was pain as flesh met unyielding wood. Raurí brought back his fist and hit the tree again and again. As the pain flooded through him the hairs retreated, the knuckle joints writhed and adjusted and the aching retreated to be replaced by agony in his injured hand. Raurí turned and stared at the wolf crouching only feet from him.

"I am not an animal," he yelled.

The wolf retreated a few paces from him shaking her head.

"Raurí, don't be afraid. Accept your life and your destiny."

The wolf's muzzle changed shape and the head altered as the forehead became more prominent. As Raurí witnessed the transformation taking place, he could stand no more. He turned and stumbled from the fairy grotto, blindly banging into trees in his distress. He wanted nothing more than to get away from that thing that crouched upon the ground and talked to him and told him he was not Raurí Mac Cathail anymore but an animal replacement.

"I am human!" he yelled as he burst from the cover of the trees.

He ran down the fairy hill, tripped and fell, and rolled and tried to stop, putting out his injured hand and feeling the pain as it hit the ground and he could not stop his forward momentum until he came to the bottom. Raurí got groggily to his feet and stumbled forward; wanting to run from that cursed place but winded and injured he could manage only a shuffling trot. Behind him an animal cried out. It sounded like a wolf or a dog howling but Raurí could hear his name mingled in with that yowling.

"Raurí, come back, Raurí Mac Cathail, come back."

CHAPTER NINE

"Raurí, Raurí."

Someone was slapping his face.

"No," he groaned, "It's not true. I am a man."

"The poor fellow's delirious. He's talking gibberish. Help me carry him in the house."

Raurí opened his eyes.

"Damian."

"Raurí, what happened?"

His uncle Ivor bent over him.

"You gave us a fright staggering into the yard like a drunken donkey."

Raurí stared around him at the familiar yard and the house.

"I'm home."

"How did you get here? You're in a right mess; your clothes dusty and you all sweaty. Why didn't you send word? I would have come and fetched you."

"I... I couldn't wait. Had to get home. Fed up with lying abed and those females fussing over me."

"I would have thought you were having the time of your life being tended hand and foot. You probably missed your Uncle Ivor's home cooking. Let's get you up to the house."

On unsteady legs with Ivor on one side and Damian on the other they went indoors.

"Lie down on the settee and rest. I'll make a pot of tea."

Ivor went in the back to get the tea, leaving Damian and Raurí alone; Damian hovering awkwardly, shifting from one foot to the other. Now and then he would grin uncertainly at Raurí.

"Damian, sit down. You're making me nervous hopping about like that."

"Oh Raurí, it's so good to see you home again."

Raurí lay staring through the window, watching the thick cumulous clouds drifting across the sky. He could remember little of the journey home. Stumbling along roads, his mind a blank, not wanting to think of what had happened in the fairy ring.

"I am a man," he whispered.

Damian's keen ears picked up the whispered phrase.

"What is it Raurí? You kept repeating that when I found you lying out in the yard. Of course you are a man. Why wouldn't you be a man? Are you thinking of the people who beat you up? There were probably too many of them for you to handle. It's no shame on your part you couldn't stand up to them. Just because you couldn't fight all of them don't make you less a man."

"You don't understand, Damian. It's nothing to do with the attack on me. It's something else altogether." Raurí stared speculatively at his friend.

"It was you that brought me to Ina Riley's. When I was unconscious did I say anything?"

"I don't think so. There was one time you were feverish and leaping around in the bed. I had to hold you down. Ina tied a blanket around you to keep you from harming yourself. You sure scared me, Raurí. You were howling like a banshee."

"Howling!"

"Yeah, it may have been that nightmare you were having. The wolf dream you had."

"Yes, I remember... the wolf dream..."

Ivor arrived carrying a large teapot in one hand and dangling three mugs from the other, interrupting the conversation.

"Fetch the milk and sugar, Damian."

The three men sat in the parlour drinking strong sweet tea and making small talk.

"Maybe you won't need me now Raurí is back," Damian remarked at one stage.

"Hell, Damian I hadn't thought about it," Ivor replied. "How do you feel about it? Do you like the work?"

"Sure I like the work, Mr Ivor." Damian reddened and stared at the floor. "I never had a job before."

He trailed off, not able to tell Ivor how much the job had increased his self-esteem and how important it felt to come to the creamery and work there.

"Leave things as they are for now. Raurí's in no fit state, anyway. We'll have a think about it when he feels well enough. And anyway who's to know what is going to happen when the war starts."

Raurí was not really paying much attention, his own woes at the forefront of his mind.

"War, the bloody war has started already," he said. "It started a couple of years ago when Germany invaded Belgium."

"Not that war, you gombeen. There's a bunch of madmen in Dublin collecting arms and recruiting men. I know them all, or at least some of them—Clarke and Pearse and Connolly."

"Who are they going to fight?"

"The fools want to take on the British Army unless someone stops them."

"But the British are already at war with Germany."

"Yeah, and that's what might just push these zealots into their own war. They think that while the English are distracted fighting the Germans they won't have the wherewithal to tackle a rebellion in their own backyard."

"You're mad, Uncle Ivor. Nobody could be that foolish. Aren't our Irish boys over in France with the English. They're being slaughtered in droves. Nobody would stand for these fanatics in Dublin with their madcap uprising and our own chaps fighting and dying in France. It would be like stabbing them in the back. Where is their patriotism?"

"Their patriotism is rooted in the past and the rebellions that took place with monotonous regularity ever since the English invaded Ireland seven hundred years ago. Every generation has their share of dreamers and schemers. These fellows believe the time is right for Ireland to rise up and throw off the English yoke."

"Nah, it will never come to that. Only an idiot would think of taking on the British Empire. They'd wipe out any uprising without breaking into a sweat."

"You know that, and I know that, but the mad boogers in Dublin don't know it. I have it on good authority the rising is to take place come what may."

Raurí stared at his Uncle Ivor. The discussion of a possible rebellion had pushed his problems into the background. He knew his uncle well enough to realize he would not make up a thing like this.

"How do you know they are getting ready for an uprising? We're a long way from Dublin."

Ivor smiled that wry smile of his.

"I was approached by the Irish Volunteers. Everyone knows I was a sergeant major in the British Army and fought in the Boer Wars. They asked me to train their men. They're building an army and need experienced ex-soldiers for the job of instructing the recruits."

"I'm sure you told them where to go."

His uncle was gazing into his mug, avoiding looking at his nephew. Raurí stared hard at Ivor, his suspicions roused.

"More tea anyone?" Ivor asked.

"What are you not telling me? You're hiding something."

Ivor grinned sheepishly at his nephew. Raurí turned to Damian.

"Do you know anything about this?"

Damian shrugged his massive shoulders and would not look at Raurí.

"Tell me it's not true."

As he pondered the consequences of a possible uprising, his own experiences faded into the background.

"I have often heard you argue against an uprising, Uncle Ivor. Why don't you take your own advice?"

"I have argued until I'm blue in the face and they still won't give up the idea. They never tire of telling me England's disadvantage is our advantage. While England is distracted by the war against Germany they won't have the resources to throw troops into Ireland."

"And now you're helping them?"

"They're just country boys, Raurí. All they know is looking after cattle and pigs and cutting turf. They need someone to train them. It might at least give them a slim chance of survival if it ever comes to fighting." Ivor suddenly grinned. "I couldn't refuse. They made me a major. Me a goddamn major—Major Foyle!"

Raurí stared at his uncle, digesting this disconcerting news. As he pondered on the implications, a glimmering of an idea was taking shape. It seemed they were all agreed an uprising against the master race would be suicide.

As a consequence of the brutal beating that had almost killed him, Raurí's reasonably tranquil life had been thrown into disarray. Then there had been Aishling's devastating revelations back at the fairy circle.

He had tried to dismiss the episode as an implausible dream but the more he thought about it the more he worried the fantasy might have some truth in it. He had to acknowledge the transfiguration of Aishling into a wolf might not have been a trick of the imagination but a real event. According to her, he was tainted by the same curse of bestiality. He looked down at his hand and saw the bruises and cuts where he had battered it against the tree and remembered Aishling's words.

"Raurí, you must listen. It is for your own survival. You can't go back to your old life without knowing what has happened to you. Have you heard the term werewolf?"

He was suddenly afraid—afraid of what he had become—what he might become. Perhaps it would be better to die—to be killed in some mad and glorious adventure rather than live as a fiend—half-man half-beast. Dead, he would be free of such a fate.

"Werewolf," he whispered.

"What was that you said, Raurí?"

"Have you got room for another Volunteer?"

CHAPTER TEN

The orders came to Ivor via courier—a local youngster who arrived at the creamery on his bicycle, out of breath and filled with self-importance. Raurí wasn't there at the time; he was out with the cart delivering milk and cheese to the railway station for transport to Dublin. Ivor was inside the shed tending the churns. Damian was in the milking parlour with the cows. The youngster poked his head inside the creamery.

"Major Foyle," he yelled and Ivor looked up.

"Aloysius, whatever brings you here at this time of the day?"

"I have a message for you, sir."

"A message, come on, let's go up the house."

Inside the big kitchen Ivor poured the lad a mug of creamy milk from a large jug.

"Now what is this message?"

Aloysius pulled a crumpled envelope from his jacket pocket.

"Here, sir."

While the messenger drank his milk Ivor opened the envelope and read over the single sheet of paper.

"Mmm... I wonder what that means. Do you know what is in this letter?"

"No sir. As you know I'm a member of Fianna Eireann," Aloysius replied, mentioning the youth organization formed as an Irish alternative to Baden Powell's Boy Scouts. "I just deliver the letters. Why, what's it about?"

"I'm not sure. I just hope it doesn't mean what I think it means."

"Where is Captain Mac Cathail?" the youth asked as he set down his empty mug.

"Captain Mac Cathail—where did you hear that name?"

"Sure everybody's talking about Raurí and his promotion. I just wanted to see him and shake his hand."

Ivor laughed.

"You did, did you? He's at the railway station. You might meet him on your way. This is Easter Saturday and the end of Lent. Were you good during Lent and what did you forswear during that time?"

"I gave up swearing and smoking, Major Foyle."

"Smoking! What's a youngster like you doing smoking?"

"I'm twelve for goodness sake!"

Ivor had to turn away to hide his smile.

"What are you doing over Easter—anything special?"

The boy's face brightened.

"We're for the seaside. Old Mick Damon says the weather is to be fine all weekend. Ma's packing a picnic and we are heading for Blackrock."

"In that case she'll want a piece of cheese to put in the sandwiches. Come with me."

Out in the creamery Ivor handed his messenger a bulky muslin-wrapped bundle.

"Now don't you be eating holes in that on your way home."

The boy's smile was mischievous.

"I might have a nibble to stop the hunger."

"On your way, you imp. And watch out for the peelers. Don't let them catch you with any of these letters. If there's any chance of them stopping you, bury them envelopes in the bog or eat them along with the cheese."

"They won't catch me. I'm too fly for those boyos."

Ivor watched the lad pedal out of sight, and then went towards the milking sheds. Damian was busy with one of the cows, spurts of white milk jetting into the bucket underneath. He gave Ivor his lopsided smile. The milking shed was steamy from so many cows penned in one place, giving off a musty odour of animal mixed with the fusty smell of straw and dung and raw milk. Ivor leaned against a stall and told Damian what was in the letter he had just received.

"Raurí and I have been ordered to parade in Dublin, Easter Monday."

His fingers still working on the cow, Damian leaned his head against the side of the cow.

"Are they going to do it?"

"I fear so, Damian." Ivor sighed, a troubled look on his face. "If anything happens I've left papers and such in the dresser putting you in charge of things."

Damian turned his face and pushed it against the cow, not saying anything, his fingers no longer teasing the milk from the udders.

"Don't go, Ivor."

"Damian, we took an oath of loyalty to the Irish Volunteers. We are bound by that oath."

"It'll be a slaughter."

"Nobody knows that better than me. Don't forget I served in Africa with the British Army. England can't afford to allow rebellion in its own backyard while the war drags on in France. They'll divert enough force to crush us and then carry on with the fight against Germany. The Volunteers are made up of inexperienced youngsters with a sprinkling of veterans like me. We don't even have proper arms. We are going up against one of the most powerful nations in the world. A flea like us biting it on the ass will be but a minor irritant. A quick pinch between finger and thumb and it will be as if we never were."

The sound of a cart outside interrupted Ivor. He reached over and patted Damian on the shoulder then left him. Damian remained immobile listening as Ivor greeted Raurí.

"Raurí, how was the trip?"

"No problem. The stuff is safely on the Dublin train on its way to Grenville Dairy."

"Good. I've just received some news. We've been ordered to parade in Dublin come Monday. Here, let me help you with the horse."

"Monday, damn it all, it's Easter. Half the company's buggered off for the weekend. I can't see us getting a full muster. What the hell were they thinking of?"

"I tell you what they're thinking off, if I read the signs right. It's the uprising come at last."

"Uprising—they're serious then—the Irish National Volunteers are going to take on the British Army?"

"That's how I read it, Raurí. I'm, sending out word for the company to meet up at the railway station for the train to Dublin."

"What about weapons? Are we going to fight the British with hurly sticks?"

"There will be rifles and ammunition waiting for us in Dublin. We'll collect the arms and march to The GPO in O'Connell Street. We'll be given further orders on arrival."

"So it's come at last."

●　●　●

"Dunlow Place. Who knows the city well enough to take us to Dunlow Place?"

The men had disembarked from the early morning train and the thirty young recruits gathered outside the station, awaiting orders.

"I know where that is, sir." Tim Royston, thin and wiry stepped forward. "My aunt Maureen lived in Dublin and we used to visit when she was alive."

"Private Royston, you will be our forward scout. Form up, men. We will march to Dunlow Place where we will collect our arms."

The company shuffled together forming up an untidy line.

"Is that how I taught you to fall in?" Ivor roared."Do it properly. Let's show these Dublin jackeens how the men from the seventh can conduct themselves. You are soldiers. Behave like soldiers."

When he was satisfied with the line-up, Ivor motioned to Private Royston.

"Forward march."

They started off in good order, young men excited by the extraordinary adventure in which they were privileged to partake. Some wore items of military uniforms, foraged from wardrobes that held remnants of uniforms once worn by men either deceased or too old to fight. The majority wore their Sunday best and marched proudly with polished boots and firm stride.

Raurí had been promoted to captain, and strode out to one side of the column with his Uncle Ivor on the opposite flank. The first signs of trouble came when Raurí saw the dozen or so policemen blocking the street. Ivor called for the company to halt and stepped forward to the waiting police.

"If you gentlemen would see your way to moving aside, we wish to proceed along this road."

The policeman was taller than Ivor and heavily built. His square handsome face glared belligerently at Ivor.

"Well do you, now? And where, may I ask are you going?"

"You may not ask. Since when was it the task of the police to harass men on a day's outing?"

The police sergeant pushed his neck out, glaring at Ivor. Usually when he did this men flinched and stepped back. The man he confronted did not draw back but stared steadily at the policeman.

"Just turn around and march right back to the pigsty you crawled out of before I order my men to break a few heads."

"Sergeant, you may be a big man against women and children as you proved back in 1913," Ivor replied scornfully. "We don't frighten that easy."

Ivor was referring to the labour strikes a couple of years ago when police charged workers demonstrating for better pay and conditions. Police lines viciously attacked anyone unfortunate to be caught up in the melee. Men and indeed women and children who were out supporting the strikers were beaten indiscriminately, many severely injured and needing hospitalization.

The big sergeant blinked. For the first time in his career he was being stared down. He gave a signal to his squad. The policemen drew wooden batons.

"I hope you brought bandages with you, mister, for we're about to break a few heads unless you about turn and march back up that street. You have two minutes and then the blood will flow."

The sergeant caught a movement out of the corner of his eye and turned to see a dark-haired youngster step towards him. He opened his mouth to warn him and then saw the revolver in the young man's hand.

"We are marching down this road now," Raurí said quietly. "We can march over your dead bodies or you can slink off back to your kennels and lick your bollix while you still can."

Sergeant Leopold Delaney felt the rage rising in him. No one had ever spoken to him in that manner. His station in life, his size and his vindictive nature meant people walked warily around him, including his superiors. He looked into the eyes of the youth for a sign of nervousness or indecision and found none. The sergeant suppressed a little shiver. The eyes that stared back at him were cold, and gave no clue to what the owner was thinking. For a moment—for a fleeting moment—he imagined an animal of some nature stared back at him from those flinty eyes. The sergeant's anger and humiliation battled with his instinct for survival. He was fairly certain he would not survive this confrontation unscathed. And he wisely chose the bully's way out and backed down.

"I'll be watching for you, young fellow. Your days are numbered."

Red in the face and quaking with suppressed anger, Sergeant Delaney turned to his men and made a dismissive gesture. Still clutching their batons and aching to use them on these country yokels who dared to come into Dublin City, the policemen reluctantly stepped to one side. They marked the men who marched past, scrutinizing faces and filing them for future reference when they would have their revenge.

Ivor's company marched proudly on, led by Captain Mac Cathail. It was a triumphant parade, for hadn't they just faced down the feared Dublin police?

Raurí could feel the change in the company. The young recruits stepped out with heads held high and vigorous step, confident in their supremacy. They had just won their first skirmish. They were here to fight the British, whether it was the Royal Irish Constabulary or be it the British Tommy, it mattered little.

Raurí glanced across at his uncle. Ivor grinned back at the youngster and winked. That was more than enough for Raurí. He put back his shoulders and held his head a little higher as he marched forward; knowing that what he had done had enhanced his prestige with the men. They had watched while their captain faced the enemy and forced him into a humiliating climb-down.

Never before would any in their company have dared to speak to a member of the RIC in the way that Raurí had. Notorious for their heavy-handed use of batons, you kept a respectful tongue in your head when dealing with police.

Perhaps this rebellion might succeed after all, Raurí was thinking. Once his men were armed there would be no stopping them until they had chased the British out of Ireland. And then he noticed Private Royston pointing down to the right.

"We're here, sir. This is Dunlow Place."

"Company, right turn."

In good order the column marched into the street of Regency houses. An elderly gent, immaculately dressed and carrying a silver-tipped walking stick, came to meet them.

"Good morning, gentlemen, I'm glad to see you. Keep on to the bottom of the road and turn right into the entry. There's someone waiting there to issue your arms. How many more are there?"

"This is it, I'm afraid. There was some confusion about the timing of the parades and many of our fellows took off for the day. No matter, sir, we'll give them a bloody nose at least."

"That's the spirit. I only wish I was going out with you. Not as spry as I used to be. Good luck. I'll be at the top there, keeping a lookout for army activity."

The old man shuffled back up the street.

"You heard the man," Raurí called. "Let's go and get our guns."

CHAPTER ELEVEN

The arms they were promised was a pathetic half a dozen ancient rifles. Raurí distributed them amongst his band amidst much grumbling.

"There'll be more rifles when we arrive at our battle stations," he assured them. But even he did not believe it.

"Move out," he commanded.

As they marched through the streets of Dublin their low spirits evaporated in the bright sun blazing down with increasing intensity. Someone burst into song and others took it up. They were still singing when they turned into O'Connell Street.

A crowd had gathered outside the Post Office and a man in the uniform of an officer was standing on the steps with papers in his hand speaking to the crowd. Raurí called for his men to cease singing and they came to a halt to stand waiting in respectful silence in front of the General Post Office. They all knew who it was addressing the crowd. Patrick Pearse, poet, schoolmaster and a major leader of the uprising. They were just in time to listen to the proclamation by the leaders of the rebellion of their bid for independence. It was a sunny Easter Monday morning in the year 1916 when Europe was convulsed by an ongoing war that was seemingly consuming the youth of the world.

"We declare the right of the people of Ireland to the ownership of Ireland, and to the unfettered control of Irish destinies, to be sovereign and indefeasible. The long usurpation of that right by a foreign people and government has not extinguished the right, nor can it ever be extinguished…"

While the man on the steps of the Post Office was speaking Raurí was examining the building. Windows had been broken out and riflemen could be seen at the openings. Sandbags were piled in front of the door and around the steps and he wondered at the temerity of these men, himself included, to declare war against England with so few men and little or no resources. All they had at their disposal were light arms. Heavy weaponry was nonexistent. Even rifles and pistols were in short supply with some men relying on captured arms to equip themselves during the fighting.

The speech finished Commander Pearse saluted smartly and went back inside. There was a scattering of applause from the civilians mixed with a few boos and catcalls.

"Wait here," Ivor called and hurried up the steps.

The sentries saluted as they let him past. The people in the crowd took note of the newcomers and some gathered around to gawk at the company of armed men.

"What's going on?" a well-dressed man in a suit asked Raurí.

"Didn't you listen to Commandant Pearse?" Raurí answered. "It is an uprising of the Irish people to throw off the yoke of British oppression."

"British oppression my ass," a shabbily dressed woman interjected. "My Padraig is over in France fighting for the likes of you cowardly bowsers. Are ye going to fight him as well when he comes back?"

"We are not fighting the Irish people; we are fighting the foreign forces occupying our country."

"That's foolish," the man in the suit stated. "As this lady so rightly says, our own young men are fighting in France alongside our English brothers."

"WE DECLARE THE RIGHT OF THE PEOPLE OF IRELAND ...."

"We want our independence and we want it now," Raurí replied stubbornly. "As an independent nation we could make our own decisions and have control of our own fate. As it is we are at the mercy of faceless bureaucrats in London who don't give a horse's shit about how we live and have never set foot in the land they rule."

"Sure didn't our own gorgeous King George come to Dublin in 1912, ye gobshite," the shabby woman with a son in France spluttered. "I remember how beautiful the king looked in his grand carriage. We waved our flags and cheered; my own darling Padraig and me. By God, didn't the Guinness flow that day. We sang and drank till we fell over. That's what the English have given us—King George to reign over us and make us proud to be a part of the British Empire."

To Raurí's relief he caught sight of his uncle hurrying down the steps of the Post Office.

"We've had our orders," Ivor declared. "We're for St Stevens Green to reinforce the defences there."

"Yer a crowd of gobshites," another woman who had been listening in to the exchange screamed shrilly. "Wait till the soldiers start on ye. Ye'll be messing your britches, then. Sheila's right. My man is over in France fighting. If he was here now he's knock some sense into yer bloody thick skulls. God save the King!"

"Forward march!"

"God save King George. Down with the Irish Volunteers."

"God forgive ye for rising up against your rightful king. God save King George."

The company started off followed by insults and boos and catcalls as more people joined the bawdy woman. By the time they were out of earshot, the previous euphoria had dissipated. St Stevens Green came into view and the company straightened shoulders and marched with renewed eagerness. There was a row of vehicles which had been overturned to form a barricade across the road. An officer saluted Ivor.

"Reinforcements, I presume."

"Major Foyle reporting for duty, sir—Seventh Laois Company."

"We're busy barricading the approaches. We have men digging trenches." The officer pointed with his revolver into the park, then glanced around Ivor's little squad. "They look as if they can handle a spade. Take half your squad into the green and help with the digging. The rest come with me."

Ivor counted off half the squad and put Raurí in charge of the remainder. Raurí saluted his new OC.

"Captain Mac Cathail, sir."

"Let's go. There's no need to tell you to keep your eyes peeled for the British. We need to look at our defences and spot any places that need attention."

As he turned to lead them on a circuit of the Green, shots rang out. There was a cry of pain and Martin O'Conner crumpled to the ground, a red stain appearing on the front of his shirt.

Bullets were striking the roadway and some ricocheting into the air. Raurí had his gun in his hand, casting round for the source of the firing. He saw movement at a window in a tall building overlooking the park and fired towards it. His shooting had no effect on the barrage of lead pouring down from the building.

"Can you see where the firing is coming from?"

"That hotel across the road there."

"The Shelbourne."

They fired at the windows of the hotel. Raurí's men had scrambled for the dubious safety of the park by clambering over the iron railings. Martin O'Conner lay where he had fallen.

"Captain Mac Cathail, get someone to help you carry that poor man to the medical station. I'll keep their heads down."

Raurí ran across to the downed man. The red stain had soaked a large wet patch on his shirt. He wasn't sure if O'Conner was dead or not. Raurí heaved him upright before throwing him across his shoulder. He knew he could not climb the railings with his burden so he ran along the perimeter looking for a way in. Bullets pinged all around him as he ran. Raurí imagined the soldiers or whoever was firing from the hotel windows poking a weapon outside and shooting without exposing themselves. There was a small gate ahead and he dodged through, startling the men crouched inside.

"Have we got an infirmary?" Raurí panted, "I need a doctor."

Hands were reaching out to help.

"This way."

An officer came rushing up.

"We can't hold the Green, we're too exposed," he yelled

Even as the man was speaking bullets were whipping into the shrubbery as the firing continued from the buildings overlooking the park. Raurí, helped by a fresh faced young volunteer, hurried along carrying his wounded comrade.

"We haven't got a doctor but we have nurses," the soldier told him.

"They're very good. He's not dead, is he?"

"I hope not. He's one of my men. The firing started almost as soon as we arrived. Martin was hit in the first volley."

They ran awkwardly across the road carrying their burden. A couple of young girls, attired in white aprons and white hats and wearing Red Cross armbands, waved them inside a building.

"Bring him in here."

There were already two casualties inside the makeshift infirmary.

"On the table there," a nurse ordered.

They did as instructed, grateful to lay down their burden. Just then there was a burst of firing from outside and Raurí could hear bullets striking the front of the building. Grabbing his revolver he rushed to the front door and crouched in the hallway, trying to spot where the firing was coming from. He could hear a female voice swearing and risked a peep outside. A young woman in nurse's garb was lying on the ground by the park gate while the street was being sprayed by bullets.

"Bloody British. I'm a bloody nurse, for god's sake."

The bullets continued to rain down on the street.

"Get ready," Raurí yelled. "I'll keep their heads down. See if you can make a dash for it."

He squatted in the doorway and fired up at the hotel. As Raurí put shot after shot into the windows he could see glass tumbling down bouncing off the windowsills. The firing into the street eased. In the lull he could hear someone screaming. There was a sudden patter of feet on the street and the nurse dived through the doorway. In her hurry she crashed into Raurí sending him flying. For a moment all went dark and he thought he had been shot.

He could feel someone breathing into his ear and then he was brushing a mass of hair from his face and could see again. He looked into the grinning face of the young woman, her hair cascading down—enveloping him—soft and smelling of lavender. He grinned back. She made no attempt to move. She licked his ear.

"Thank you my handsome rescuer."

"Davina! Leave that soldier alone. There's a poor fellow here with a bullet in him. We need your help."

Raurí felt her weight easing off him, sweeping back a mass of dark hair that reached to her waist. Then she was gone inside the room where the wounded were being treated.

"Davina," Raurí murmured as he crouched in the doorway peering up at the hotel, "let's hope we meet again."

A hail of bullets peppered the door. Chips of granite cut into his face as he ducked back. Raurí bobbed back outside and let off a few more shots. His shooting was beginning to have its effect, for the marksmen had to shoot from well inside the rooms, affecting their accuracy. Bullets hit the pavement and the roadway instead of in and around the doorway. Raurí could feel wetness on his face and when he put up his hand it came away red with blood where the stone chips had splattered him.

"Well maybe I blooded some of them as well," he reflected.

He heard shouting from the park and looked up to see what was happening but the shrubbery was blocking his view.

"You there in the infirmary," someone called.

Raurí could make out a figure crouching amongst the bushes. He waved back.

"I hear you."

"We're to regroup. Our boys are being cut to pieces out in the open like this."

"I thought you had trenches dug?"

"They're not much use seeing as the buggers are sniping at us from the roofs. You're to regroup in the Royal College of Surgeons. We stand a better chance of defending that than stuck out in the open."

"Royal College of Surgeons—where the hell's that?"

"Clockwise from where you are, it's about three hundred yards. We'll give you ten minutes to get ready and then we'll give you covering fire."

This conversation was interspersed by sporadic firing which intensified now that Raurí was not firing back.

"Oh dear God!' The exclamation came from the messenger crouching in the bushes. "I'm hit."

"Stay where you are," Raurí shouted. "When we evacuate, I'll come over for you."

"Ten minutes."

The voiced was strained. Then silence. Raurí fired a few rounds at the snipers before retreating back inside. The infirmary smelt of lanolin and iodine and blood and sweating bodies. Raurí instinctively looked for Davina. She was hunched over Martin, working on his bloodied chest.

"Got it," she exclaimed and held up forceps. "Here, wash it and put it in his pocket in case he wants it for a keepsake."

The long hair that had enveloped Raurí was tied back with a strip of bandage. Her white apron was smeared with blood and some was on her cheek and Raurí thought she was the most desirable woman he had ever seen—perhaps with the exception of Aishling; but then Aishling was far away and Davina was here in the midst of battle.

"We're to evacuate to the Royal College of Surgeons," he called. "We've got ten minutes or less and then they'll give us covering fire."

"My hero," Davina said and gazed at Raurí with large amber eyes and he was lost in admiration as he gazed back at her.

"I... aw, ten minutes..." he said, hesitant as the full impact of her gaze worked on him.

"Ten minutes," she repeated then turned and clapped her hands, breaking the spell. "You hear everyone; we got ten minutes before we break out of here and get to the Royal College. We'll need someone to carry poor Martin O'Conner. I need volunteers."

Raurí stepped forward.

"I'll carry Martin."

Davina put her hand out and gently pushed him back.

'No, darling, you'll be out in the hallway shooting the hell out of anything that shows its ugly British head."

Raurí watched admiringly as she organized the evacuation.

"Sally, you and Alice are in charge of the walking wounded. Moira and me will carry poor Martin here though he shouldn't be moved. If he survives all this he deserves to live until he's ninety."

Suddenly everyone was busy. Raurí hurried back to the door to stand guard once more. Davina came up behind him.

"I've had an idea we can go out the back and find a safer route to the College. When we're ready you come inside and join us."

"I can't. There's a wounded volunteer in the park. He brought the order for the evacuation and got a bullet for this trouble. He's out there now. I can't abandon him."

Impulsively she stepped forward and flung her arms around Raurí. He smelt blood and the hint of lavender. Her lips were on his soft and warm. They stayed like that for what seemed a very long time. When she eventually released him, her eyes were dreamy and at the same time slightly misty.

"You keep safe, my beautiful Raurí Mac Cathail. We have a date you and me, at the Royal College."

CHAPTER TWELVE

Raurí estimated more than the stipulated ten minutes had passed before the firing started up across the park. He waited a moment or two more and emptied his revolver up at the snipers.

"Take that you lousy bastards," he yelled, and ran across the road and into the park.

He flung himself into the bushes where he reckoned the wounded man was hiding.

"Where are you?" he yelled.

Bullets were whizzing around him like angry bees and Raurí forced himself to ignore the danger. He caught glimpse of a leg outstretched in the dirt and pushed through the shrubbery. The messenger was lying on his front. Blood had seeped through his tunic. Raurí quickly dropped to his knees beside him.

"Hey, fella, you're safe now."

As he was talking Raurí turned the man over. He was unresponsive and Raurí put his fingers beneath his jaw, feeling for a pulse. Finding none he placed his head on the messenger's chest listening for a nonexistent heartbeat. Martin stared at the dead man's face, a great sadness seeping through him.

"Damn it, you're not much older than me."

All the time he knelt there, bullets continued to splash through the foliage and the sound of gunfire intensified all around St Stevens Green. Raurí thought of the young nurses attempting to get to a place of safety under such severe conditions. He had to join them and pushed through the bushes towards the college. Something stung his arm but he did not stop.

His expertise in moving undetected came in to full play as he wormed his way through the undergrowth without disturbing the foliage. The snipers who had originally spotted him were still firing into the place where he had found the young messenger, unaware their target had moved on. Raurí arrived opposite the college.

"Hello!" he yelled.

There was no response.

"Hello, Captain Mac Cathail here."

Again there was no response and he reckoned the gunfire was drowning out his shouts.

"Damn it, I'll have to risk it. I can't stay out here. It's only a matter of time before I'm hit."

He waited for a lull in the firing then swiftly vaulted the park railings into the road. Bullets splattered all around him as he sprinted across and flung himself at the big doors.

"Let me in," he yelled, battering on the door with the butt of his revolver.

As if to assist in his efforts to gain entrance, bullets peppered the thick wooden door.

"For god's sake, let me in!" he hollered, tensing his body against the expected impact of a bullet.

He turned and putting his back against the door fired his revolver in the general direction of the shots coming at him. As the hammer clicked on empty the door suddenly opened behind him and someone grabbed him by his collar and yanked him inside. Off balance Raurí went down and found himself staring up at an officer.

"You're hit."

"Huh?"

"Your arm is covered in blood."

Raurí looked down and his sleeve was a wet mess of redness.

"I didn't feel a thing."

"Get yourself to the infirmary and have that arm seen too."

"The infirmary—did the nurses make it safely then?"

"Yes, they all made it safely. They told me you stayed to save a wounded comrade. What happened?"

"He came across the park to tell us to evacuate and was hit. By the time I got to him he was dead."

"I'm sorry. When you get yourself patched up come back and report to me."

Raurí made his way along the corridor towards the infirmary looking forward to seeing Davina again.

"Raurí!"

She rushed across and nearly hurled him back through the door again as she flung her arms around him and hugged him fiercely. She had on a clean tunic and Raurí was concerned he might stain it.

"Ah... careful, I'm bleeding," he said, even as he relished the feel of her eager body pressing against him. "You'll get blood on your apron."

"Oh my poor darling. Come on over here."

The room smelt of blood and sweat and chemicals and was busy with young women wearing Red Cross armbands and white aprons working with the casualties. Davina led Raurí over to a chair and helped him take his jacket off.

"What happed to the chap you went to rescue?"

"He was dead when I got to him."

"Poor Raurí."

Her hand rested lightly on his check before she become brisk and efficient. Davina cut away his blood-soaked shirt. There was a gash in his upper arm where the bullet had creased him. It was still bleeding and now that he had stopped running Raurí could feel the pain.

"It's not too serious," his nurse murmured. "I'll clean it and bandage it and you'll be fighting fit again."

When she finished dressing the wound she helped him on with his jacket and put her arms around him.

"Just you be careful, Raurí. Come back here so we get to know each other better."

Her kiss was warm and prolonged and then she was turning back to tend the casualties while Raurí headed back to report for duty.

"We found a store of rifles when we took over the college," the officer informed him "I want you to take one and join your unit up on the roof."

Ivor and the rest of the company were crouched behind a low stone parapet running along the front of the roof. The men were taking it in turns to rise up and let off a few shots before ducking back again. Raurí came out on the roof and crawled over to his uncle.

"Thank goodness you're all right," Ivor yelled above the noise of gunfire. "I was worried about you."

"So you should be."

Raurí indicated the bandage on his arm.

"Is it bad?"

"Nah, only a scratch. I got rescued by a bevy of beautiful nurses. They were fighting over who got to dress the wound."

Ivor roared with laughter and punched Raurí's good arm.

"Martin O'Conner is in the infirmary. He doesn't look too good. Got one in the chest."

"Yeah, there are three of our men down already and two missing. I've seen bodies lying out there in the green. No one can get to them. Those bloody snipers are making it too hot."

"Well, let's return the compliment and give them a taste of their own medicine."

"Just be careful. Some of them are damn good."

The remainder of daylight was spent exchanging shots with the English soldiers. The main shooting was coming from the Shelbourne Hotel and the United Services Club. Night closed down over the park but the fighters could not relax. Their opponents kept up a constant barrage of sniping so that even in the dark it was dangerous to rise up above the protection of the parapet to fire back.

"Supper," a female voice was calling.

A young woman was setting a huge kettle on the roof. She reached back down through the skylight and brought out mugs and then platefuls of sandwiches.

"About time, I'm starving."

There was a scramble for the food.

"Is there a Captain Raurí Mac Cathail here?"

"Yeah me?"

"You're to report to the infirmary. Apparently you got a wound needs dressing."

"Are you sure?" Raurí asked.

It seemed too soon for his dressing to be changed. The girl shrugged; her features indistinct in the gloom.

"That's the message from Corporal Noonan."

"Corporal Noonan?"

"She said she dressed your arm earlier but she was concerned you needed it redone. She's worried about infection or something."

"She!"

The young woman looked with pity at Raurí.

"Yes, she, Captain! Corporal Davina Nolan! Women are fighting in this war too, you know."

And Raurí understood immediately who Corporal Noonan was.

"Of course, of course, I'll come straight away."

He grabbed up a thick sandwich before turning back to the men on the roof.

"Major Foyle, you heard what the nurse said. I have to report to the infirmary."

"You said it was only a scratch."

But Raurí followed the young Cumann na mBan nurse down into the building.

Corporal Noonan was all efficiency as she greeted Raurí. She glanced around the crowded infirmary. The nurses had taken over one of the lecture rooms and converted it into a makeshift hospital ward. Benches and desks had been commandeered from other rooms and converted into beds. Raurí estimated there were roughly a dozen or so casualties, mostly men but there was a young Cumann na mBan having a bloodied shoulder dressed.

"It looks a bit crowded in here," Davina observed. "I'll take you to another ward."

Munching on his sandwich, Raurí obediently followed his nurse as she led the way back out into the corridor. Davina stopped at a door, turned her head to Raurí and winked.

"Your own private ward, Raurí."

She dragged him through the opening and locked the door behind her. The room was dim but he could make out a bed in one corner. Her arms were round his neck and she was hugging him fiercely. There was fire in his veins as he responded. The noise of gunfire faded and there was only their need for each other.

CHAPTER THIRTEEN

"What the hell," Raurí yelled at his uncle, as they crouched behind the parapet and bullets whistled overhead and cascaded against the brickwork. "How can they do that? They must have a whole battalion occupying the Shelbourne Hotel."

"Machine gun—we haven't got anything to match that. There will be a pause when they change the ammunition belt. All we can do is fire off a few shots when that happens."

"Machine guns! They'll slaughter us if they bring up any more of those."

"Water cooled Vickers machine gun. Can fire four hundred and fifty bullets a minute. There's not that many issued yet, so hopefully that's the only one we'll have to deal with."

"One's enough," Raurí yelled back.

The machine gun never let up and the college was sprayed with a constant stream of bullets punching holes in barricades and keeping everyone under cover. At one stage heavy explosive thumps were heard within the city.

"Now what?" Raurí asked.

"Artillery shells. Coming from somewhere near the Liffey. Eighteen pounder sounds like."

"Artillery!"

The heavy thumps continued.

"My guess is they brought a gunboat up the river and are lobbing shells into the city. It's only a matter of time now. We have no weapons to match machine guns and artillery. Even our homemade bombs are more of a danger to our men than they are to the English."

For Raurí, the main danger was the machine gun and he resolved to do something about it. When he got the chance he went in search of the officer in charge.

"You're stark staring raving mad."

"All I need is a couple of men. The smaller the party the better. We'll stand less chance of being detected."

All around them could be heard the splatter of machinegun bullets striking the building and penetrating the windows as the makeshift barricades were shot to pieces. The distant thump of shelling went on unabated.

"Three of you, you say to do the job. It's suicide, you know. How can I justify sending you out to die."

"Even if I stay here inside this building there could be a bullet with my name on it. I've already been hit once. I'll be just as dead if I get killed outside. At least I would have died attempting something to help win this war instead of sitting here helpless."

"Okay, choose your men and pick your time to go."

Raurí went in search of Corporal Noonan. He found her in the kitchen cutting bread. It had to be sliced thinly to make it go further.

"Captain Mac Cathail, how nice to see you. Have you come to help?"

Raurí patted his wounded arm.

"My arm's throbbing a lot. I was worried about it. Could you have a look?"

Davina laid down her knife.

"Mmm... we'd better have that seen to. I've got the very remedy for your condition."

In the afterglow of their exertions they relaxed in each other's arms, lazily content.

"You're a hairy monster, Raurí," Davina murmured, idly tracing her fingers through the matted hair on his chest.

Some of Raurí's euphoria seeped away. He had gone to war thinking it would be an antidote to the poisonous thoughts of what might have happened to him. However, he could not ignore the changes in his body—

his keen eyesight and sense of smell and hearing. Even the increase in strength had not gone unnoticed. When he had rescued Martin O'Connor from the Green on Monday he had picked up the wounded man, surprising himself by the ease with which he carried him to safety.

Raurí had imagined in the excitement of the war he could leave his nightmares behind, but everything he did seemed to remind him of what he might have become. And now Davina had hit on one change that more than anything else bothered him.

"You could be a throwback, Raurí—a real caveman."

"Why do you say that?"

Raurí failed to keep the apprehension from his voice, hating what she was implying. Davina rolled on top, her own soft hair, gently caressing Raurí's face.

● ● ●

Under cover of darkness the three men slipped out into the Green, each armed with a revolver and a knife. They also carried homemade bombs in tobacco tins with a stub of fuse protruding from a hole drilled in the side. Before they left Ivor smeared soot on their faces.

"Come back safe."

"Don't drink my ration of Guinness," Raurí warned him.

With Raurí leading the way, the three men crept along the perimeter of the park. Tristan Donnelly was a pimply faced youth who had volunteered to accompany him along with Vivian Sheehy a man in his mid twenties, solid and reliable.

The plan was to get behind the Shelbourne Hotel and find some way of scaling the building and get to the machinegun that was doing so much damage. Five Volunteers had been killed and another three wounded along with a young Cumann na mBan who had ventured out for additional medical supplies thinking her Red Cross armbands would protect her.

Raurí crept to the road and peered through the bushes at the buildings opposite. There was an opening further along and he pointed to it.

"That should take us back of the buildings and we can make our way along to the Shelbourne. I'll go first and if there is no alarm you follow."

All three made it safely into the entry and headed for the hotel. Suddenly Raurí put up a hand and the little band stopped. He could smell tobacco. His caution was rewarded and he saw the glow of a cigarette.

"Wait here."

The whole plan depended on stealth and surprise. Raurí slid out his knife. It had a horn handle and was razor sharp. His Uncle Ivor had handed it to him before they left on their mission.

"I brought that knife back from Africa. See you keep it safe."

"There might be blood on it when you get it back."

"As long as it's English blood."

Like a shadow of the night Raurí drifted forward, his revolver loosened in the holster but he didn't want to use that or it would mean the end of the mission. The assault had to be stealthy until they reached their objective—the machinegun on the roof of the hotel.

Tobacco smoke strong in his nostrils, Raurí could see the dark shape of the sentry. The man was lounging against the wall, the butt of his Lee Enfield between his feet with one hand gripping the long barrel and the other holding a cigarette. Raurí was but a couple of strides from his target.

As Raurí leapt forward, the soldier sensed movement and turned his head. He opened his mouth to shout but before any sound emerged the dagger plunged into his throat. The sentry gave an odd gurgling sound and sagged against the wall. Raurí hugged the man, keeping the rifle between them so that it would not fall clattering to the ground. The soldier twitched and jerked in his arms and blood spurted out from that terrible wound in his neck.

Raurí could feel the hot blood spilling on to him and some splashed on his face. He could smell and taste the blood and Raurí had an almost uncontrollable desire to open his mouth and take in some of that bloody liquor.

He closed his eyes and kept his mouth tightly shut while he held the soldier, convulsing in his death throes—hugging the dying man as a brother might hold his sibling to comfort him in his last moments. But Raurí's motive was not to console but to keep his victim from making a noise that would alert his comrades.

There was a sigh as the man in his arms expired. Raurí lowered him to a sitting position. He placed the rifle in an upright position between the man's legs so that a casual observer might imagine the sentry still on guard but doing it sitting down.

"Okay," he hissed, "let's hope there are no more guards about. This is the hotel. Let's see if we can get to that bloody machinegun."

CHAPTER FOURTEEN

The courtyard behind the hotel was deserted. Raurí could hear the harsh stutter of the machine gun as it spewed its deadly missiles at the Royal College of Surgeons. Raurí examined the walls and noticed the handgrips set into the brickwork ascending the side of the hotel.

It was now Friday night and the fight had been going on since Easter Monday. Along with the racket of the machinegun could be heard the thump of shells being lobbed into the various buildings occupied by other small groups of Resistance Fighters. The English gunners were using incendiary bombs and massive flames lit up the skyline as the city was slowly engulfed.

"I think we've found our way to the top," he called.

"It's a hell of a way up, Captain."

Raurí was peering up at the skyline. He reached out and grasped a rung.

"When I'm halfway up, Vivian, you come on after me. Tristan you wait here. Keep well hidden around the side there. If anyone comes and it looks like we might be discovered kill them."

Raurí climbed up the side of the building, hand over hand, heading for the roof and hoping the brackets went up that far. Below him he could hear Vivian labouring after him. As he got higher he was able to look out over the city and for a moment he paused as he took in the extent of the fires raging across Dublin.

"My god," he murmured, "looks like the whole city is on fire."

And indeed as far as the eye could see, colossal flames were shooting into the sky like a volcano spewing its burning debris into the night. He wondered how many of the men and women fighting in the city had died under that fierce barrage of shells.

With renewed determination, Raurí resumed his climb and arrived at the guttering running around the top of the hotel. Taking out his revolver Raurí cautiously poked his head over. With some relief he realized there was no one on the roof. He could hear the machinegun stuttering out its deadly hail of death but could not see it. A glass skylight about four feet high ran across the roof, blocking his view of the front of the hotel where the machinegun was positioned.

Quickly he stepped on the roof and crouched there, his revolver at the ready and waited for his companion to join him. Raurí could hear Vivian's heavy breathing before he arrived at the top. His head come into view and he peered anxiously at Raurí.

"Okay, it's all clear."

Vivian pulled himself the last few feet and crouched on the roof beside Raurí.

"Uncle Ivor told me it takes six men to man the machine gun and there'll be other soldiers up here as well—snipers and suchlike. Let's have a look-see."

They crept to the skylight and peered across, all the time acutely conscious of the rate of fire of the machinegun. The crew manning the gun were crouched over their deadly weapon at the edge of the roof. The gunners were protected by sandbags. On either side were snipers. There was a pause in the firing and there was a buzz of activity as the gun crew set about the task of changing the belt.

"What are we going to do, Raurí? There's far too many for us to take on."

"What the hell you mean? There are only ten."

"That's odds of five to one—five to bloody one."

"We've got surprise on our side."

As he spoke Raurí was pulling out the tobacco tins loaded with explosive.

"We lob the bombs at them. That should take care of some of them. Then before the survivors recover we finish them off."

Vivian was pulling his bombs from his pockets but Raurí stopped him.

"You go to the other side of the roof," Raurí told him. "That way they'll have to shoot at two separate targets."

Obeying Raurí's orders, Vivian took up his position on the opposite side. Raurí was wishing he had brought Tristan up on the roof as well. It did seem the odds against them were loaded.

He pulled out a stub of a candle and lit it with a match. Raurí looked over and saw Sheehan's candle flickering in the darkness with the man like a grim shadow of death crouching over the flame.

Raurí cupped his hands around his tiny flame; shielding it from sight as a signal to his companion he was ready to go. He lit the fuse of his first bomb and watched it fizz to make sure it had taken and hurled it towards the front of the roof. It landed behind the gunners who were too busy to notice.

Raurí lit another bomb and tossed this one towards the snipers also. He had his revolver in his hand and fired at the machine gunners. One man went down and his companions turned to him assuming he had been hit by fire from the Royal College. At that moment the tobacco tin puffed out a tiny flash and a cloud of smoke. The gunners looked in bewilderment at this phenomenon, wondering how the thing had got there. Just then

...AND HURLED IT TOWARDS THE FRONT OF THE ROOF.

Vivian fired. Another man went down and it was only then the soldiers realized they were not alone on the roof.

The soldiers were swivelling around, searching for the source of the firing and spotted the intruders behind the skylight. One more bomb fizzed and spluttered nearby while the others that should have ripped into the soldiers causing chaos and death also failed to explode.

There was a sudden outburst of shots as the soldiers turned their weapons on their attackers. The skylight exploded and shards of glass cascaded down into the rooms below, leaving Raurí and Vivian exposed. Raurí dropped flat, still firing but it was finding it difficult to line up targets with bullets winging all around him and ricocheting from the roof and the frame of the now glassless skylight.

Out of the corner of his eye he saw Vivian standing and firing steadily at the soldiers. Raurí turned to yell at him to get down when his companion staggered back his body jerking as lead poured into him. The Volunteer crumpled to the roof leaving the gunners to turn their attention to the remaining raider.

Raurí fired and rolled and fired and rolled, hoping he was moving fast enough to avoid a bullet. The raid was doomed. The bombs that were supposed to do so much damage were a miserable failure and now Vivian was dead and it looked as if Raurí was shortly to follow.

As his revolver clicked on empty Raurí somersaulted into the opening that had been a skylight. He tumbled into the room below, landing on his feet with the crunching of broken glass beneath his boots.

Wildly he looked around him, his senses probing for danger. Nothing stirred in the room and for the time being he was safe. But Raurí knew the soldiers would soon arrive at the wrecked skylight and take shots at him.

In desperation he ran to the window. Not bothering to try opening it, he booted the frame and glass tinkled out into the street below. Raurí stood on the windowsill, looking down and knew he would never survive the drop. When he looked up and knew instinctively that was the way he had to go. Raurí resigned himself to the knowledge he was going to die either way.

"Dammit, I can still take a few of them with me."

Raurí leaned back out into the night, holding onto the window frame and looked up. About four feet above him he could see the ledge that ran along the top of the hotel. He looked down again at the street. He had to leap from the window and grip the ledge and then lever himself up on to the roof where English soldiers would be ready to gun him down.

He leapt.

For a few fateful seconds he reached desperately, his hands clawing for a hold on the rough stone—his legs swinging free—hands slipping—swinging back and forth like a man hanging on the edge of a cliff and the street four stories below—pulling himself up purely by the strength of his arms and his head came over the ledge and just above him was the parapet.

All he had to do was let go with one hand and grasp the top while holding onto the ledge with his other hand—his legs wildly kicking—reaching desperately for a grip and missing and his arm being torn from the socket as his weight swung free—the street below with iron railings placed to impale him when he fell and soldiers waiting on the roof to fill him with lead.

His fingernails tore and he tried not thinking of the fall and concentrated only on getting over those few feet of stone and onto the roof. And somehow his fingers found purchase and his feet kicked against the window and he pulled his body over the parapet and rolled onto the roof and lay there gasping and staring up into the sky wondering why he was still alive.

Raurí gained his feet, gazing around him, breathing heavily; the noise of gunfire loud in the night air. The soldiers all lined up before him. Only they weren't looking at him. They were firing into the room where he should be, only he wasn't there but against all odds was on the roof behind them. Raurí grabbed for his revolver. He knew he had only moments to live. The weapon was not there. In his mad scramble to get back on the roof his weapon had been lost.

"Damn!"

Raurí looked around for a weapon thinking the soldiers had left something he could use and the machine gun was sitting there unattended while the gun crew screamed profanities and raked the room below with rifle fire thinking they were exterminating the man they had seen leap inside. Raurí grabbed the barrel of the machinegun and immediately let go as the heat seared the skin on his hands.

"Holy mother!" he yelled.

In desperation he wrapped his arms around the middle of the weapon where the tripod joined it and heaved. The gun was incredibly heavy and took all Raurí's strength to lift.

His muscles straining, Raurí hefted the gun in his arms. He almost went down again before he got the weapon turned around. It was then the soldiers sensed something was amiss or caught movement behind and turned.

"See how you like it," Raurí yelled and squeezed the trigger.

They were turning to run when the gun sprayed out its lethal missives of death. Raurí swivelled the gun on its pivot and forgot the pain in his burned hands as he took vengeance for the loss of his comrades who had fallen to that deadly weapon.

A few soldiers escaped as they did what Raurí had done and leapt through the ruined skylight but most of them died as the heavy bullets punched them into oblivion.

With no more targets, Raurí ceased firing. He caught a movement over to his right swivelled the gun in that direction. A trapdoor was open and the head and shoulders of a uniformed man emerged. He had a rifle in his hands and was turning his head around, obviously bewildered by what was happening on the roof. Where he had expected a gun crew and his comrades, the place was littered with bodies. Before he could make sense of the carnage, Raurí depressed the firing trigger. Once more and the deadly stream of lead spewed out, almost cutting the man in half before he disappeared back inside. Raurí ceased firing as the trapdoor was pulled closed again.

Raurí leaned back against the sandbags. He was safe for the moment while the enemy worked out a way of attacking him. But he was under no illusions what would happen.

He was isolated on the hotel roof and they would find some way of attacking and killing him. There was no way they could allow him to keep possession of the machine gun. The weapon was a key component of their attack and was effectively keeping the Volunteers penned up.

Soldiers would pop up through the wrecked skylight and via the trapdoor so he would be assaulted on all sides. They would come at him with rifles and grenades. He would survive only for a very short time against such a concerted attack.

Raurí repositioned the sandbags to give him some protection from the expected assault. And then he paused. Once he was dead, the English soldiers would take over the machine gun and resume the attack on the Volunteers. He would have accomplished nothing, only the slaying of a handful of English soldiers. He and his companions would have died in vain for he had every reason to believe that Tristan, left below on guard, would have been captured or killed by now.

"Our mission was to destroy the machine gun," Raurí spoke aloud. "That is why I am here on this bloody roof and I am about to die without accomplishing that."

He still had some of the homemade bombs which had a dual purpose of being used against enemy soldiers and were also to be employed to wreck the machine gun. After witnessing the dismal failure of the devices, Raurí knew they would be just as ineffective against the gun. The weapon looked so durable he doubted even a sledge hammer would damage it.

Raurí stared down across the park and he could make out the Royal College where Davina waited for him. He had not told the young Cumann na mBan of his mission, not wanting to worry her about the danger he would be facing.

"Davina!" he yelled, his voice lost in the din of battle. "Goodbye Davina. Remember me—Raurí Mac Cathail."

He turned from the Green and looked out into the night. Gigantic flames soared into the sky as the City of Dublin was consumed by fire. Incendiary shells could be seen arcing into the fiercely burning buildings.

Raurí turned to the machine gun and reaching down wrapped his arms around it and heaved mightily. His muscles bulged as he strained to lift the heavy equipment once more. Slowly his legs straightened. Like a colossus he rose in the night with the deadly machine of death cradled in his arms. A few staggering steps and he was at the parapet.

The weapon was his last means of defence, but it was also the enemy's means of killing his comrades and Raurí knew what had to be done. He fell against the parapet and the gun wedged on top with the tripod legs each side. He knelt and heaved with one last effort. The gun teetered on the edge and Raurí gave it one more push. It was enough. The gun overbalanced and fell out into the night to go crashing down to the pavement below. He had accomplished his mission but was resigned to the fact that he would not survive to boast about it.

CHAPTER FIFTEEN

Raurí listened to the boots shuffling along the roof. He lay on his back sheltered by the sandbags and stared up at the night sky. Clouds of smoke were making it difficult to see the stars.

"Dante's Inferno," he murmured. "We tried to created an independent state and instead have created a hell with the English stokers burning everything to ashes."

He listened to the voices coming out of the darkness.

"Can you see anything?"

"Not a bloody thing. Do you think they're dead?"

"Toss in a grenade. That'll stir 'em up."

"Nah, you know the orders. No grenades. Can't risk damaging the gun."

"To hell with the gun, what about damaging us?"

The bayonets came over the top of the sandbags, followed by helmeted heads.

"I surrender." Raurí held his arms outstretched.

"What the...!"

More bayonets—more helmeted heads staring aggressively at the youngster lying behind the sandbags.

"Where's our bloody machine gun?"

"Sorry about your gun. I was trying to pick it up but I tripped and it fell into the street."

"You rebel bastard!"

The bayonet was raised in the air. Raurí braced himself.

"Hold it! Hold it!"

An officer appeared, holding a revolver.

"Jones, look over the side see if you can spot it."

A soldier moved to the parapet and leaned out. He gave a sudden grunt and slid back to the roof.

"I've been hit," he screamed holding his arm, blood staining his fingers.

"Those bloody Sinn Feiners."

"Keep your heads down," the officer yelled, seemingly oblivious of the fact he had ordered the soldier to peer over the parapet. "Right Paddy, keep your hands where I can see them and come out from there."

Raurí did as he was bid and crawled out from the shelter of the sandbags.

"Bates—Morrison, take him down below. Shoot him if he gives you any bother. The rest of you get these sandbags up again and start shooting at those damned rebels. What a goddamn mess."

They prodded Raurí with their bayonets, swearing and calling him names.

"Keep walking Paddy sheep-shagger."

"Please Paddy give me an excuse to ram this steel up you."

At the trapdoor, as Raurí bent to clamber inside, a boot cracked into his rear end. He was catapulted inside, landing heavily on the floor where he got another kick as he tried to scramble upright. He was pushed inside a room with soldiers crowding after him all eager to hit the prisoner. The abuse only stopped when the officer ordered him to be tied to a chair.

Bruised and bleeding Raurí stared dazedly back at the officer.

"You realize the penalty for treason is hanging."

"I wouldn't know. I was fighting to free Ireland from a foreign invader."

The officer slapped Raurí hard across the face, the force of the blow making his head ring.

"This is British territory. You are under the jurisdiction of the His Majesty's Government. To make matters worse we are at war with Germany, a foreign power, and you peasants up and stab us in the back while our boys are fighting and dying to keep you rebels free."

"That's the point I was trying to make. I am at war with a foreign power..."

He got no further as the officer punched him in the face.

"Though I must admit your arguments are rather forceful and your tactics even more so." Raurí spat out blood. "Maybe you can beat me into submission. But it doesn't alter the fact that you are a foreign invader and our people will fight you until the last drop of blood."

As his interrogator was raising his fist to strike again he was interrupted by a hammering on the door.

"Captain Welland! Captain Welland!" an urgent voice was calling.

"Let him in."

An excited soldier pushed inside the room.

"They're surrendering, there's a ceasefire ordered. The rebels are asking for terms."

"Ceasefire—I hope we don't give them any ceasefire," The captain snarled. "We can pound them into rubble." Staring thoughtfully at his captive he took out his revolver. "You killed my men and destroyed a valuable piece of army ordnance. I don't think the ceasefire will matter to you, sonny boy. It's a bullet in the head for you."

He raised the weapon and placed the muzzle against Raurí's temple. Raurí tensed wondering if he could kick the officer's legs from under him. There was a disturbance out in the corridor and the captain paused, turning his head towards the noise. An officer appeared in the doorway.

"Captain Welland, have you heard the news. Those bloody Sinn Feiners are finished."

He frowned as he saw the revolver and Raurí tied to a chair.

"What's going on?"

"Ah, Major, I just heard about the ceasefire. Too late for this rebel. He's killed several of my men and threw the machine gun from the roof."

"You're not going to shoot the fellow in cold blood. No matter what he's done it's strictly against regulations to shoot prisoners."

Raurí waited, knowing his life hung by a thread. It depended on how much authority the major had over his captain.

"Dammit, he's a bloody rebel. I'd rather hang him but a bullet in the head and he'll be just as dead."

"Captain, I order you to put up that weapon. There'll be no summary executions in my squad."

Raurí could feel the tension in the room as the officers glared at each other.

"It's a court martial offence," the major spoke again. "And I'll push it to the limit."

Abruptly the barrel of the gun was removed. Raurí breathed deeply, suddenly realizing that he had held his breath while the standoff took place.

"Two of you take the prisoner and make him secure. Lock him up somewhere while the terms of this ceasefire are worked out. What's your name?"

"Captain Raurí Mac Cathail, Irish National Volunteers."

The major stared quizzically at Raurí.

"You seem a mite young for a captain. Same rank as Welland here. Is it true you destroyed our machine gun?"

"Captain Raurí Mac Cathail, Irish National Volunteers," Raurí stubbornly repeated.

"Well Captain Raurí Mac Cathail, in my army, soldiers get medals for doing that sort of thing. Take him away." He turned to the captain. "If anything happens to him I'll hold you responsible."

Raurí was thrust into a coal cellar and the door banged too, shutting him in darkness. Raurí was suddenly overwhelmed with tiredness and looked for a comfortable place to lie. A bundle of coal sacks made a rough if dirty bed and he fell asleep.

Raurí had no idea how long he slept before he was rudely awakened and roughly jostled out into the street. Across the Green he could see British soldiers gathered outside the Royal College. His guards hustled him in that direction. As they arrived the doors opened. He watched the defeated insurgents trail out of the college. Raurí looked for Davina amongst them. He saw his own company along with Ivor emerge as he was shoved roughly into the line-up of prisoners.

"Where's Davina" he hissed fearing the worst.

Ivor winked at his nephew.

"There was no one of that name in the college."

Raurí breathed a sigh of relief. Somehow Davina had managed to slip away.

Escorted by soldiers they were marched down Grafton Street, up Dame Street and in through the gates of Dublin Castle, the centre of British rule in Ireland. Around him he could hear his companions discussing their eventual fate.

"We'll be hanged for sure."

"Nah, they'll shoot us."

As they marched inside the castle, Raurí noticed uniformed police officers. They were scanning the prisoners as they came through. He recognized one of the peelers.

"Ah, that one," a voice called.

Raurí was pulled out of the line and found himself staring into the gloating eyes of Sergeant Delaney. An army captain came across.

"What's going on here?"

"This man is a notorious criminal," the police sergeant replied glibly. "He's wanted for armed robbery and murder. We've been after him for months. I'm taking him into custody."

"Oh, very well. We got plenty here to take care of. One less won't make any difference."

Delaney was smiling at Raurí.

"Who would have thought we would meet again so soon? I have a cosy little cell waiting for you."

With a policeman on each side, Raurí was marched out the castle gates. He gasped as he felt a crippling blow in the kidneys and stumbled and almost went down but was held up by the police constables.

"I have a score to settle with you," Sergeant Delaney told him. "I'm an expert at settling old scores. It's gonna to be a long and painful process."

CHAPTER SIXTEEN

They took him but a bombed out building. In the bedroom was an iron bedstead and Delaney stood it on its end.

"That should do nicely."

The constables shackled Raurí to the iron posts of the bed. Still weak from the punch in the kidneys he could not put up much resistance.

"You pair go to the nearest pub and have a drink," Delaney told the constables. "But before you begin, bring me back a bottle of malt. Interrogating prisoners gives me a thirst. Oh, and put a few bottles of Guinness with that whiskey. I'm likely to be here for some time."

The constable coughed and looked embarrassed.

"What about money, Sergeant? We ain't got any money."

"Money, what the bloody hell you want money for? We're Royal Irish Constabulary for Christ's sake. How long have you been in the force?"

"Six months, Sergeant."

Sergeant Delaney shook his head in exasperation.

"Just go and do as you're told. Don't keep me waiting."

When the constables left on their mission, the sergeant righted an overturned chair, blew plaster dust from it and removing his belt and tunic, carefully hung them across the back. He removed his peaked cap and set it on the seat.

Raurí weighed up the policeman, noting his big frame and thinking he was robust enough to have fitted in with the Phelans from his old life. And Raurí grew afraid when he saw the expression in the eyes of the policeman He knew he was going to have a very painful hour or two with this big peeler.

"Now me boyo, I want you to tell me again what you said when we met Monday last."

Raurí dropped his head and stared at the policeman's boots. They looked twice the size of a normal person's footwear. There was stinging blow on the side of his face and Raurí thought his jaw was dislocated.

"Are you deaf? I asked you to tell me what you said to me on Easter Monday."

"I said, 'oh look, they have dressed that big turd in a sergeant's uniform.'"

A thick finger prodded Raurí's chest.

"A comedian..."

Raurí tried to bring up his knee into Delaney's groin but the big man was ready and punched him in the solar plexus. All the breath left Raurí's body and he hung by his manacled wrists gasping and trying to bring his breathing back to normal. Delaney stepped back relishing his victim's distress.

"I was so much looking forward to this meeting. Your little army is finished. That lot of posers playing at soldiers are going to pay for upsetting King George. There'll be hangings aplenty afore this little fiasco is over."

He leaned forward and patted Raurí on the face where he had slapped him. Raurí flinched. His face was aching, his head was aching and his guts were aching and Sergeant Delaney had only just begun.

Rauri had a fair idea he wouldn't survive this encounter. He felt bitter that he had come through the fighting to die at the hands of this sadistic RIC sergeant. Footsteps crunched through the rubble outside. The constables had returned with the refreshments. Delaney took the whiskey in his big paw and pointed it at the prisoner.

"Strip his clothes."

"His clothes, Sergeant?"

"Are you deaf as well as thick, constable? I said strip him."

Rauri tried to fight them but Delaney pulled out his baton and beat him about the head and shoulders. After that the youngster was no match for the constables as they stripped his clothing and shackled him to the bed once more. Delaney pulled the cork from the whiskey bottle with his teeth and took a long slug.

"Okay, you two, back to the pub. If anyone asks, you were with me all day."

"Yes, Sergeant."

The constables scuttled out the door, relieved they did not have to stay and witness the brutality they knew their sergeant was capable of.

"You know, it has been a great week for me, soldier boy," Delaney said conversationally. "With all this chaos in the city, I was able to settle a few old debts; fellows that had done me wrongs in the past and females who had scorned my favours. I spent the week visiting them all. There are three dead bodies out there that have nothing to do with the rebellion. And the females. When I arrived and told them I was arresting them for supporting the rebellion they soon lost their snooty airs. And now the party's over. But I got you to play with. It will be a great finale to the week. You have to learn respect, sonny. You insulted me in front of my men. That cost me some respect. No one said anything, but I could see it in their eyes. So now you have to pay."

The sergeant punched Rauri with meticulous care; solid bone-jarring punches that seemed to damage his very organs. The pain was like nothing Rauri had ever experienced. Rauri lost count of time. He could hardly breathe he was in so much agony. His arms felt as if they had come out of their sockets as he hung suspended. When he tried to take the strain by pushing up, Delaney kicked his legs from under him. Rauri drifted in and out of consciousness. He had no way of telling how long he hung there being battered. Eventually the beating stopped and the big man moved to the chair where he had hung his tunic.

"I must step out a while to replenish the Guinness. Just you hang around here and enjoy the break. I'll be back to put you out of your misery. I must say I did not expect you to last so long. Most fellows would be dead by now and I respect that. Shows spirit and manliness. You would have made a good peeler."

Left alone, Raurí struggled feebly at his fetters, but there was no way he was going to escape the irons that cuffed him to the bedstead. He sank down in despair, trying to breathe so it did not hurt. But he was in constant pain. He tried to think about Davina and hoped she was safe. He knew he would never see her again and regretted that. Inevitably his thoughts turned to the other woman who had been in his thoughts over the weeks that had passed since the transformation in the fairy grotto.

"Aishling," he breathed the name into the dim interior of the bombed out house.

He had fled from Aishling because he could not accept what she told him he had become.

"I am a man," he whispered. "I am a man and I will die a man. I am not a beast."

The strain on his shoulders was excruciating. He pushed up with his legs, which did nothing to ease the pain. Everything hurt. He looked up at his wrists, raw and bleeding. He wriggled his fingers and struggled again to pull his hands through the iron loops that held him fast. And then the thought came and Raurí tried to push it away but it was persistent.

He saw again the human hand turning into a wolf's paw and he dared to think the unthinkable. He flexed his fingers, staring hard, imagining what would happen if he had animal paws instead of hands. He concentrated; imagining the unimaginable. The pain was unbearable. He let out a groan.

"Aaagggh."

The hairs on his hands spreading back down on to the wrists. The fingers thickening and shrinking—becoming deformed and stubby. The agony grew and he cried out again, but there was no one to hear that lonely animal-like howl.

• • •

Sergeant Delaney stepped into the street, leaving the warm cosiness of the pub. His mood was high.

"Time to put the little bastard out of his misery."

He stumbled inside the house, his big boots crunching over rubble tumbled there by the explosion of a shell during the bombardment.

"I'm back," he called. "Did you miss me? Sorry I kept you waiting but I'm here now."

He stepped inside the room where his captive was chained and considered if he should remove his tunic.

"I'm in a good mood. Drink always does that to me. I might just kill you right off. What a kind and thoughtful fellow am I."

He blinked, wondering if his eyesight was faulty. It was mid-evening and through gaping holes in the walls and roof, the light coming into the house was diffused and murky.

"What the..."

The room was empty. It was impossible. No one could have slipped the handcuffs. With a roar of rage Delaney staggered to the bedstead, peering blearily at the manacles still attached. With a frustrated snarl the police sergeant turned back to the room then stopped. He swayed slightly as he looked at the doorway. The biggest dog he had ever seen was standing in the opening. Black as night with eyes that were red burning holes.

"Are you the devil?" Delaney whispered.

The dog might have been carved from ebony, so motionless, even its breathing seemed stopped. Delaney was scared. This was not how he visualised the night's end. He had come back here to further torment his victim before killing him and burying his body in the ruins.

"What do you want?"

And the dog answered him. It seemed impossible but its lips slid back exposing rows of vicious teeth.

"You."

And Delaney knew then that Satan had come to claim him. All those stories the Christian Brothers had fed him about the devil and hell and the evil ghouls that lurked out there waiting for unwary sinners were true after all. He fell to his knees and joined his hands in an attitude of prayer.

"Jesus, Mary and Joseph, help me this night," Sergeant Delaney babbled. "I know I have sinned but I realize the error of my ways. From this night I am a reformed man. I will attend mass and go to Holy Communion and pray for the dead and..."

His praying turned to a shriek as the big animal sprang into the room hitting him full in the chest and bowling him over. The sergeant put out his hands to push the thing away and felt a searing pain as he did so. He stared at his hands covered in blood and some of the fingers missing.

"Please God help me," he bawled.

They were his last words before the wolf's jaws closed on his throat and razor sharp fangs tore the soft flesh.

CHAPTER SEVENTEEN

Aishling O'Hagan waked and saw the shadowy figure standing at the foot of her bed.

"So you came back. I heard you went to Dublin to fight the good fight. Much good that did."

"You don't seem surprised to see me."

"No, I knew you'd return. I have that effect on men. They can't stay away."

She smelt the blood.

"You're hurt."

Throwing off the covers and rising naked from the bed she stretched long and languorously. In spite of his fatigue and the hurting of his bruised body Raurí felt himself responding. The door opened and Ina stuck her tousled head around the door.

"I hear voices."

"It's Raurí; he's come back to us. Been to the wars and needs patching up."

"Mmm... seems to be making a habit of it."

Ina came further into the room and Raurí grabbed the end of the bed as a wave of weariness swept over him. The two women were immediately in attendance, supporting him one each side. Their hands gentle as they helped him on to the bed. He tried to mumble something but his words were all mixed up and waves of darkness swept over him.

When Raurí awoke he could see daylight poking bright fingers past the curtains. As he lay there he could smell the familiar herbal mix Ina had administered to his bruised and battered body and smiled. Even as he had slept the woman had tended him. Raurí arched his body and stretched and immediately winced. Every part of his anatomy was throbbing with pain and now that full awareness was arriving he could feel the aches and bruises on his body where Sergeant Delaney's fists had pounded him.

He could remember little of his flight from the war-torn city and had only hazy recall of his reception into Ina Riley's home. In spite of his aches and bruised body he could feel the pangs of hunger. Gathering his strength,

Raurí crawled from the bed and wrapped a blanket around his nakedness.

A pot of stew was cooking on the open fire and Raurí smelt the meat and herbs and vegetables and spices and his stomach rumbled fiercely. He could hear someone outside and peeked out the window.

Aishling was in the yard. Raurí stood transfixed as she sluiced water over her tawny body. The sunlight glistened upon her skin giving her the appearance of a golden statue, only this was no statue, but a very alive and extremely beautiful young woman. Raurí forgot his hurts and his hunger as another kind of hunger crept upon him.

"Aishling, how I missed you," he said aloud.

He whirled as he heard a noise behind him. Ina had entered and was soberly regarding him. She went across to the pot, stirred the mix, tasted and added salt.

"She missed you too. She would not tell me what happened, but the day you left she came back in here and I could see she was upset. When I quizzed her about you she just said you had gone back to your people."

Raurí turned back to the window in time to see Aishling drying herself and remained watching while she pulled on a simple green cotton dress, not bothering with undergarments and somehow the sight of her covered up was almost as exciting as when she was naked.

"Are you hungry?"

"I'm as hungry as a wolf," he said unthinkingly and stopped.

He turned and stared at the woman stirring the meat-laced stew, but Ina was not looking at him, absorbed in her cooking. Before he could say any more the door opened and Aishling walked inside, her animal musk only slightly muted by her libations.

"The sleeper awakes," she said. "How did you get into such a state?"

"It's a long story."

"You can tell us over breakfast."

As they ate the hot and spicy stew he told the women of his adventures, leaving out only his love trysts with Davina and ended by telling them of his imprisonment and beating by Sergeant Delaney.

"I was handcuffed to the bedstead and helpless while Delaney beat me."

"Go on, Raurí. What happened?"

He looked up, distress in his eyes, and as he spoke that same anguish was reflected in his voice.

"I changed, I changed my shape." Raurí stretched out his hands—the wrists raw and weeping. "I guess I left some skin and fur on those irons. When Delaney came back I ripped his throat out. I ripped his bloody throat out."

Aishling reached out across the table and took his hand in her own.

"You survived, Raurí. You're alive and that police sergeant is dead. That's what matters."

He lifted tortured eyes to her.

"Yes, I killed him. But the terrible thing is, as I tore his throat out I felt an excitement as if something primitive in me was lurking there all along, and surfaced in that moment of blood lust." Raurí's eyes glazed over. "A blood lust—that was it. I... I savoured the moment of the kill... a primitive lust..." his voice trailed off. When he continued talking it was as if he were having a conversation with himself. "I could have spared him. I could have left that place as soon as I was free but there was a rage in me. I wanted to kill—to destroy—to rend and rip and use my... my powers to slay my enemy. So I lay in wait and took him. He pleaded for mercy—even went on his knees and prayed... but there was no mercy in me."

"Raurí, from all you told us he was an evil man. You were right to kill him. He deserved it, more so, as he was a peeler, sworn to uphold the law and there he was using his authority to prey on others. You should feel no guilt."

Raurí's eyes narrowed and he peered across the table at her.

"That's the awful thing. I feel no guilt."

"Will they be coming after you?" Ina asked, trying to interrupt Raurí's self-recrimination.

Raurí blinked and turned his gaze on Ina.

"I guess. I killed a peeler. They won't let that pass. They'll hunt me down."

"You'll have to go on the run. They'll put a price on your head. We have to get you away to a place of safety."

"Can't I stay here?"

Ina was shaking her head.

"They'll search for you in all your old haunts. Someone will have seen you and they'll come looking." She looked at Aishling. "Have you any ideas?"

"There are deserted farms where he could hide out."

"What about the creamery?" Raurí asked. "Uncle Ivor was taken prisoner by the English. I saw him being marched with the others into Dublin Castle. We left Damian to run things until we came back. Damian can't keep running the place on his own."

"You're right; I don't give much for Ivor's chances. If they don't hang him they'll throw him in prison. Or maybe they'll just hang them all."

"There were hundreds of prisoners. Surely they won't hang them all."

"Don't you read your history? The English have slaughtered thousands of Irish in the past to keep their grip on Ireland. They're in the middle of a bloody war with Germany. Do you think they'll show mercy to a crowd of rebels? If they don't hang Ivor, they'll put him in prison where he'll never see daylight again."

"Damn, what a mess! I guess I'm lucky to be alive and free."

"Looking at the state of you, I wouldn't call you lucky."

Aishling went to the creamery and told Damien to keep the creamery going and she and Ina would come over when they could to help out. She brought back clothes for Raurí.

"Damian says to stay safe. The police came around searching for weapons but did not find anything. The news is bad coming out of Dublin. The English have started the executions. There's no word about your Uncle Ivor."

• • •

Raurí learned the police did not appear to be searching for him. There were no wanted notices and he concluded that the Dublin Authorities had not linked him to the killing of Sergeant Delaney. He decided to risk going home. When he walked into the creamery Damian looked up, saw Raurí, gave a great whoop of joy rushed over and crushed him in a bear hug.

"Any news of Uncle Ivor?" Raurí managed to ask when Damian had calmed down.

"All we know he is in prison."

"And was anyone looking for me?"

"Not a hint. The peelers came a few times and searched the place looking for guns what with Ivor being taken prisoner in Dublin. Each time they come they steal stuff and do more damage. It's taken me all my time trying to keep the creamery going with those rogues doing everything to hinder me. Just because Ivor was caught in the fighting in Dublin they think his property is fair game."

"Humph! You can't tell me anything about the peelers," Raurí said. "For now we keep our heads down and hope the RIC will not bother us too much."

There was the noise outside of a horse-drawn vehicle arriving in the yard. Raurí, went to the door and saw Aishling freeing the pony from the dairy cart. Raurí stepped into the yard and she turned and smiled at him sending a warm thrill through him.

"Hello Raurí, so the wandering Jew finally came back—welcome home."

"THERE'S NO NEWS ABOUT YOUR UNCLE IVOR."

"It's good to see you, Aishling," Raurí said, his voice husky. "How have you been?"

"Busy." She indicated the harness she was working on. "I'm afraid you're redundant now. I've taken on your job of delivering the cheese and milk to the railway station."

He laughed and she turned fully towards him and smiled with him.

"I'll give you a hand," he said, and stepped into the yard. "I missed you."

"Are you home to stay?"

"I hope so."

He reached out to help as she continued working on the harness. Their hands touched and a thrill coursed through him at the contact.

"What are you doing tonight?" he asked

"Mmm... I was thinking of visiting the fairy ring; the Hill of Gaming." She turned bright mischievous eyes to him. "The night promises to be clear of clouds so I might do a bit of stargazing."

"That sounds exactly what I was thinking of doing. I can think of a game we can play at the same time."

He was early, and sat inside the fairy circle gazing up at the sky remembering the last time he was here with Aishling. He had fled from the hill, horrified at what Aishling had shown him. But now he accepted his dual life. Something breathed on the back of his neck.

"Something wondrous this way comes," he said and a pair of arms encircled him and pulled him to the ground.

"Did you miss me?" she asked.

"Yes, you were always on my mind. When the going got rough I had the memory of our times together and that brought me solace."

"You're an awful liar. I bet you say that to all the girls."

"Only the ones lying on their backs with me on top."

She giggled and pulled him close.

"Shall we undress?" she whispered in his ear.

It took only moments for them to disrobe. He ran his hands over her lithe body.

"You're almost more beautiful than I remember," he managed to say before their lips met.

Afterwards they lay together, staring up at the sky which was indeed clear and starlit as she had predicted.

"You've changed" Aishling said. "You seem more at ease with yourself and more mature."

"It doesn't frighten me anymore. I am what I am."

She stretched luxuriously beside him and he was aware of the change coming over her. It triggered his own response and the familiar prickling of his skin as the hairs erupted on his body. There was pain as the joints altered and his bones shifted but it was a hurting that was in a strange way also pleasurable. His transformation was much swifter now.

Even so, his companion was quicker still, and he gazed in wonder at the sleek golden animal prowling around the enclosure. Aishling in turn was in admiration of the powerful wolf that Raurí had become. She noted the muscular shoulders and thick legs and the dense black fur covering his body.

"You are truly king of wolves," she growled.

"If I am king then you are queen."

She leapt nimbly at him and nipped his ear then turned and padded to edge of the trees.

"It is a good night to run."

She glided from the shelter of the trees and loped gracefully down the slope. He followed and together they ran, glorying in the power of tireless limbs and the wildness in their hearts. It was the first of many such trysts and though they took care not to be seen, rumours began to grow of the sightings of shadowy, wolf-like creatures glimpsed occasionally by late night revellers. The tales grew with the telling and the creatures became hellish beings that breathed fire and left a trail of burnt grass behind. When sighted, they vanished in a puff of smoke amidst the smell of brimstone.

In December Ivor was released from prison and returned home. That Christmas was a happy time for them all. It was to be the last such peaceful celebration, for forces were gathering on the horizon which would bring a terrible time of slaughter and brutality to the peoples of Ireland as they tried to shrug off the burden of their powerful neighbour that had won the war in Europe and could now turn the might of her armed forces on the tiny nation lying in its shadow.

CHAPTER EIGHTEEN

Raurí was working with Damian in the creamery when they heard the lorry grinding along the road. There was no need to look outside for they recognized the sound of the police wagon.

"Here we go again," Raurí said.

Raurí was in charge, for Uncle Ivor had gone to Dublin to purchase parts needed to repair machinery and to consult with the leaders of the resistance. The pals listened, hoping the lorry would go on by, but it was futile hope as the vehicle turned into the yard.

"More bother."

Raurí went out into the yard to greet the police. There were seven in the squad and they jumped down from the lorry with rifles held ready.

"Afternoon." Raurí greeted them. "Have you come far?"

He didn't need to ask, for the unit were from the Mullentoone Barracks and two or three times a week they came to the creamery and demanded drinks and pocketed cheeses and anything else lying around. The sergeant was a bull of a man with blunt features, small eyes and a mean spirit.

"We're looking for the rebel, Ivor Foyle. Get him out here at once."

"He's not at home at the moment. Perhaps I can help."

"Are you a rebel too, ye gobshite?"

It was always the same. The policemen would interrogate Ivor, and then search the house and outbuildings for weapons or seditious literature. They never found anything, for Ivor was careful to keep any incriminating materials well away from the creamery. More often than not they broke things and made free with any edibles that were available. After a few such visits Ivor hid valuables and kept the best cheeses out of sight. Everyone hoped the police would tire of the game and eventually leave them alone.

"I don't have any interest in politics. I prefer a night out at a *ceilidh* and a few jars of Guinness," Raurí answered. "I suppose you like a jar and a dance yourself, Sergeant?"

Sergeant Maguire reached out and grabbing Raurí's shirt pulled him close. Raurí could smell the bad body smell and a foul breath. Raurí had to stop himself from reacting and doing something foolish like hitting the sergeant.

"You messing with me, sonny boy? I could take you in for questioning."

The sergeant sensed movement behind Raurí as Damian came out to support his friend. Raurí was thrust to one side.

"What the hell are you looking at you goddamn freak?"

Sergeant Maguire drew his revolver and stepped towards Damian. Raurí sucked in his breath and tensed. He kept a wary eye on the policemen lounging against the side of the lorry, watching with amusement the antics of their sergeant. Raurí picked out which one he would tackle first should the sergeant show any inclination to shoot Damian.

Damian cringed away as if he were terrified of the policeman. Raurí knew different. The sergeant would find he had indeed a monster on his hands, for Damian was strong as a plough horse and Ivor had taught both Raurí and Damian fighting skills that needed no weapons. The sergeant raised his gun and swiped Damian across the head. He scrambled away squealing like a pig and danced across the yard.

"Ah, don't hit a poor crater like me," he cried, cavorting and turning cartwheels and grinning like an idiot.

The policemen were laughing and Raurí relaxed as he realized Damian's clowning had taken the heat out of the situation.

"Bloody monkey," Sergeant Maguire growled.

He strode across to the lorry making sure to shoulder Raurí out of the way as he passed.

"Back in the lorry."

Once the police tender had disappeared down the road Raurí came across to Damian.

"Are you hurt?"

"Sure I needed that tap on the head."

"What are you talking about?"

Using both hands, Damian framed his oversize head.

"Everyone knows I got water on the brain. A tap on the head is the very thing to drain it off."

Raurí reached out and grasped Damian's shoulders.

"I always suspected you were bloody mental. Now I know for sure."

And then they were both laughing. With his arm around Damian's shoulders Raurí marched back inside. It was evening before Ivor arrived back from his trip to Dublin. Raurí was sitting with Damian in the kitchen having dinner when Ivor walked in.

"Uncle Ivor, you must be hungry."

Raurí jumped up from his meal to serve his uncle.

"Thanks, Raurí."

Ivor nodded to Damian in greeting. Damian poured tea and Raurí set a steaming plate of potatoes and bacon and cabbage before him.

"Ah man, am I ready for this."

"How did the trip go?" Raurí asked, as he resumed eating.

"The war starts all over again."

"Humph, did it ever end. The RIC certainly don't think so. They're arresting and beating up our boys so it is risky to go out for a drink nowadays. They walk in a pub and kick in a few heads thinking we'll put up with it forever. Then they demand drinks as if it was their God-given right."

"Well the people in Dublin have given us new orders. We're to start hitting the police. We're to give them a warning and if they don't stop their raids they're be declared traitors and shot."

Raurí punched his fist in the air.

"At last! Those gobshites will regret messing with us. Only today Maguire came by with his pack of hounds and pistol-whipped Damian here." He chortled. "Tell Uncle Ivor the joke about the tap on the head."

Damian grinned sheepishly.

"I said the tap on the head would cure my water on the brain."

"You're a right pair of jokers. But to more serious things. We have to plan a raid. Any suggestions are welcome. But the priority is to get weapons. Phelan has been smuggling arms in but we have to pay a premium price for them. I've been given leave to use the authority of the Provisional Sinn Fein government to pay for them. We're to give them a promissory note to that effect."

"Yeah, we lost a lot of good weapons in Dublin during Easter week, and good men too. The men will be harder to replace."

"Will Phelan let the weapons go without cash up front?" Damian asked. "They're only interested in making money. I wouldn't trust them the length of my coat sleeve."

"We'll see about that." Ivor looked grim. "If they defy an order from the legitimate government of Ireland then they could be regarded as traitors."

"Benedict Phelan wouldn't give a pinch of snuff for the legitimate government of Ireland. Like I say he's only interested in profit. If Dublin Castle asked him to supply the RIC with arms I dare say he would only be too happy to do so. He is only interested in lining his pockets."

"We've nowhere else to go." Ivor sighed. "Dublin can't supply us with arms—they're short enough as it is. But they're convinced the fight will be won out in the countryside with brigades raiding and attacking RIC barracks so they will be forced to go on the defensive. Then we'll force them to the negotiating table."

"Don't be too sure of that," Raurí said doubtfully. "Look what happened when we fought them in Dublin. They thought nothing of bombarding us into submission. They all but destroyed Dublin to bring us down. Those bastards don't give a damn about human life. They'll more than likely grind us into the bog when we go against them."

"Well that's settled. I'll go to Phelan and negotiate for a supply of arms. Then once we get the guns we'll strike. Have any of you a target in mind?"

"Huh, we don't have to look too far. The peelers at Mullentoone Barracks would be my first choice. Sergeant Maguire and his bully boys need to be taught a lesson."

• • •

"A promissory note! You expect me to let you have weapons for a useless piece of paper. If I come to you and ask for twenty or thirty of your finest cheeses and gave you an IOU, would you let me ride off with a cartload of cheese and milk? I don't think so, Major Foyle."

Phelan thrust the paper back at Ivor. "Take this and go wipe your ass with it. Provisional Government! You want guns you come up with hard cash. Not bits of worthless paper. I got guns aplenty. I got rifles and revolvers and grenades. The place is awash with arms since the war ended. I can hardly cope with the amount of ammunition coming in. I got the connections see. While you were fighting your stupid war in Dublin and then dossing about in an English gaol I was working hard bringing in contraband. I work bloody hard for my money and like any businessman I expect cash for my efforts. So booger off and come back when your bloody Provisional Government can give me pounds—English pounds not Sinn Finn imitation money."

Ivor's face was tight with anger.

"Is that your final word?"

Phelan didn't bother to answer but turned and walked away, leaving Ivor staring after his retreating back. There was nothing for Ivor to do only clamber back on his bicycle. He had come to Phelan, fully confident he would be able to make arrangements for the purchase of arms. Instead he cycled back to his creamery with nothing, only a dull weight of anger.

"Where's his patriotism?" Raurí stormed." Doesn't he care the peelers are roaming around the country beating, and shooting people and gaoling them? Surely they come to his place and harass him and his smuggling operation."

"Don't be too sure of that," Damian put in. "Phelan will be paying them to leave him alone."

"You're probably right. I'll have to send word to Dublin. See what they want us to do. Maybe they can send us the funds to buy the guns from Phelan. I don't hold out much hope for that. They're desperately short of money."

"Well we'll just have to keep on training without weapons," Raurí said glumly. "The men aren't too keen to keep that up for long and who can blame them. They want action. People are asking what they voted for. They voted for Sinn Fein and now all they are getting for their loyalty is a lot of grief from the peelers and the army. They're asking when the Volunteers will act. If this isn't resolved soon we'll be looking at a lot of desertions."

That night when he was with Aishling, Raurí told her of the problems his brigade was facing.

"Without those arms we're snookered. We can't move against the peelers or the army with just a few shotguns and a couple of pitchforks. In the next few days Ivor is off to Dublin again to see if he can raise the funds to pay Phelan."

Aishling lazily traced a heart shape on Raurí's chest pushing her finger through the thick hair.

"Why don't you just take the arms from Phelan?"

"What do you mean?"

"You're supposed to be soldiers. Why can't you raid Phelan and commandeer the guns? Tell him you are taking them in the name of the Republic of Ireland."

Raurí smiled at her naivety.

"There are a lot of reasons why we can't. For a start we don't know where he keeps the arms."

"If you make love to me again I might let you into a little secret."

They made slow gentle love in the grassy glade then lay in contented silence.

"This secret you promised if I made love to you?" Raurí eventually asked.

"I have a good idea where Phelan has his arms dump."

CHAPTER NINETEEN

The brigade rolled up to Enda Moloney's small farm. Moloney had a pension from the days he worked at Dublin Castle. He had retired to the country and farmed in a small way growing hay and barley and potatoes and turnips. He also ran a refuge for donkeys. Raurí had reconnoitred the smallholding a few nights ago and knew exactly where everything was.

The donkeys were kept in a paddock a few fields distant from the house. Raurí hoped to round up the animals and leave on their mission without disturbing anyone. The plan was to use the donkeys to transport the hijacked arms across country, avoiding the roads and the chance of being discovered by police or army patrols. He had considered asking permission, but Raurí could not be sure where Moloney's loyalties lay and feared the man might betray them.

"Patrick, keep a watch towards the house in case the old bugger wakes," Raurí ordered.

The gang sauntered towards the donkeys, each man carrying a rope halter. The animals had been asleep, standing in one corner of the field; a cluster of dim shapes in the starlight.

"Spread out," Raurí instructed his men. "Try and keep them in that corner until we get the ropes on them."

The donkeys were stirring, one or two heads lifting and gazing in the direction of the raiding party.

"Good donkeys," someone called, "we've come to liberate you. You have been imprisoned by a Dublin Castle lackey and exploited by British capitalists. But you need labour no more for slave wages. Join the Irish Republican Army and work for no wages at all."

Someone giggled and Raurí, sensing the growing agitation of the donkeys, hissed a command to be quiet. But it was too late and a donkey brayed noisily—the call echoing across the fields. More and more of the alarmed beasts gave voice, building to a raucous crescendo of discordant bawling.

"For God's sake," Raurí yelled, his voice hardly heard above the clamour and realising his plan for a clandestine liberation of the beasts was now impossible. "Get the ropes on them before we waken the whole neighbourhood."

Whooping gleefully, with lassos at the ready the raiders rushed forward, alarming the beasts even more and their braying went up several notches. The field became a scene of wild activity as the donkeys tried to evade their captors. Raurí managed to snare a beast, dropping a noose over its head. It immediately went wild, bucking and kicking and dragging him across the field. He dug his heels in trying in vain to halt its progress.

All around him was a frantic movement of dark shapes as the donkeys kicked out at the raiders and galloped around the enclosure seeking escape. Men swore and cursed and chased after them while the donkeys made a racket as only donkeys can, rendering the night hideous with their clamour.

Raurí was so busy trying to tame his animal he did not notice the lights coming on in the house a couple of fields away. Patrick, whom Raurí had set to keep watch, was so engrossed watching the antics of his comrades, he forgot all about the owner of the donkeys. He never heard the man who came up behind him and clouted him on the back of the head, putting an end to his sentry duty. Moloney concealed himself in the hedge, pointed his rifle in the air and fired.

The shot startled everyone, including the already distressed donkeys. They continued their frantic braying and bucking while the men who were trying to catch them instinctively dropped to the dirt.

"Come out of that field," Moloney roared, "or the next bullet is in someone's brain. I'm counting to five and if you don't give yourselves up, this useless gobshite you had on guard here gets a bullet in the head. If you've harmed any of my donkeys then you're all dead."

"Is that Enda Moloney?" Raurí called.

"Who wants to know?"

"It's the Irish Republican Army. We're commandeering these donkeys in the name of the Republic of Ireland."

As he spoke Raurí was wriggling closer to the hedge where he was sure Moloney was hiding. There was a sudden flash and a crack and a bullet buried itself in the dirt beside him.

"Move again, sonny and you'll be a dead IRA soldier. What's your name?"

"Captain Raurí Mac Cathail. Look, we don't mean any harm to your bloody donkeys. We have bicycles and we'll just have to use them seeing as you object to us borrowing the beasts."

"What are you transporting?"

"We're distributing food to poor widows and wives whose men are in English prisons."

"If you don't come out of that field with your hands in the air, there'll be a few more widows needing aid."

Raurí was angry and frustrated. His first independent mission had ended in fiasco. The little band of IRA soldiers straggled to the gate, their hands in the air where they gathered awaiting Moloney's next move.

"Leave any weapons inside the gate and come out here where I can see you."

They did as ordered. Raurí noticed Patrick sitting on the ground massaging the back of his head.

"Mitchell, you're on a charge. This will probably mean a court-martial," he growled.

"It's all right for you," Patrick mumbled. "I got a lump on the back of my head the size of a spud."

"Pity he didn't hit you harder, then we wouldn't have to bother with a court-martial," Raurí responded.

Moloney stepped into view, rifle at the ready.

"I'm calling a truce for now. Will you fellas behave yourselves?"

"Yeah, I give you my word," Raurí agreed.

The rifle barrel slanted towards the ground.

"Come up to the house."

Despondently the raiders trudged up to the farmhouse. When they were inside they were able to examine their captor. Enda Moloney was a small dark man with a smudge of a moustache on his upper lip.

"There's a kettle there and a bucket of fresh spring water. If one of you can poke up that fire we'll have tea and discuss this like civilized people. Let me look at that head."

The small kitchen was rather crowded, but soon there was a more relaxed atmosphere as tea was distributed. There weren't enough mugs and some had to share. Moloney took a towel he had soaked in cold water and told Patrick to hold it against the bump on his head.

"Now tell me what this is all about, and I want the truth this time."

"We were going to pick up a load of guns and we need to stay off the main roads. Someone suggested using donkeys for cross-country. We weren't going to harm them. We'd have returned them once we got the arms safely stored."

"You say your name is Mac Cathail. You wouldn't by any chance be related to a certain Ivor Foyle?"

"You know Uncle Ivor?"

"I knew his sister, Mary Foyle before she married Enda Mac Cathail."

"That was my mother and father. How come you knew them?"

Enda Moloney dropped his gaze and stared into his mug of tea.

"I was a rival for her hand. Your father was the better man. When they died in the boating accident I never forgot her."

"You knew my mother. What was she like?"

"She was a lovely woman. When I lost her to your father there was no one else for me. Seeing you has brought it all back. Perhaps I can save her son from this foolhardy venture."

"I know you worked for Dublin Castle. How do we know you won't turn us in?"

"I could not betray Mary's son. Tell me your plans."

"We're short of guns and I have a scheme to get hold of a few. It requires some way of transporting them and that's where the donkeys come in."

"And where exactly are these guns you're after?"

"I can't disclose that."

"I can't see how I can help if I don't know what you are planning. I promise you, anything you tell me will be confidential."

"I was going to confiscate some contraband and leave the smuggler a promissory note in the name of the Government of the Irish Republic."

"There is only one crowd of smugglers around here, and that's Phelan's crowd. Irish Republican Army or not, Phelan will not give up the guns without a fight. They will think nothing of gunning you down."

"We can still do it," Raurí said, defensively. "We have guns if there's trouble."

"I've just seen them: a couple of shotguns and a revolver. If Phelan is smuggling arms, don't you think he'll have the pick of those weapons? Phelan is well known for settling grievances with extreme violence and won't hesitate at murder. Take my advice and give up this mad venture."

"We want to fight back, but without arms we are no match for them." Raurí stopped. "You probably know better than me what goes on."

"Indeed I do.

There fell a silence between them. The donkeys had quietened, with only the occasional heehaw.

"Can I have your word you won't go squealing to the peelers?" Raurí said eventually. "After all you have told me, I don't want to be your enemy."

"Never your enemy, Raurí Mac Cathail, never that. You have rekindled old memories and feelings I thought were dormant long since. I always regretted I could not save your mother, but now there is a second chance for me. I have an opportunity to help her son. You can have the use of my donkeys on one condition."

"Yeah, and what would that be?"

"I come with you."

Wary of leaks, Raurí had kept the location of the smugglers' cache to himself. However Enda Moloney refused to help until Raurí disclosed all details of the proposed raid.

"Phelan uses an ancient chapel. There are superstitions attached to the place which keeps people from nosing around in it."

"Yeah," Moloney said. "I know the place. How did you find out about this? I imagine the location of the arms cache is a closely guarded secret."

"I have my methods," Raurí replied enigmatically.

Moloney was as good as his word and took them into the donkey field and helped put halters on the animals. They gathered the herd on the road, ready for the journey when Moloney excused himself and went back inside the house. He was missing for some time and Raurí was worried the man had gone out the back and was even now informing the police about the men who were stealing his donkeys. Raurí was about to go after the man when much to his relief Moloney reappeared and the raiding party were able to set out.

The trek across country went well and the donkey brigade arrived at their destination without incident. Raurí went ahead to scout around the site of the abandoned chapel. Satisfied the place was clear Raurí ordered his men forward.

"Moloney, you stay here to keep the donkeys quiet while a couple of us go up to the chapel to look for the arms. The rest of you spread out around the building and keep a sharp look out until I call you to load up."

In the dark, the raiders stumbled up to the ruined chapel. It was indeed an ideal place to run a clandestine operation—the ruins of the old building rising in the darkness like the carcass of a gigantic beast—eerie and menacing at the same time.

"Patrick, you come with me to help search the place. And keep alert this time."

Both men had a lantern apiece, and once inside the gloomy building they lit up. Colum's companion also lit up a fag, the tang of tobacco mingling with the dank smell of overgrown weeds that had taken over the interior of the ruin.

Raurí raised his lamp high and looked around. An owl hooted somewhere outside and was answered. The owl hooted again and this time Raurí stopped to listen, his heightened senses telling him there was something not quite right about the sound. Again he heard the owl and knew it was no natural owl call. There came sudden yell out of the night and Raurí immediately doused his lamp.

"Put out your light," he called urgently.

Just then the donkeys joined in the uproar and with men shouting and donkeys braying it sounded as if a furious confrontation was taking place. Raurí drew his revolver and moved quickly to an opening in the outer wall. He peered into the night seeing nothing that helped him piece together what was happening. And then a shotgun went off followed by more gunshots.

Raurí stepped outside and moved quickly and silently in the direction of the shots. The confused shouting continued and the donkeys were vying with each other to see which could bray the loudest. The noise covered any sounds Raurí made. He was swearing under his breath wondering if they had been ambushed by police or army or Phelan's men. Then he ceased to wonder as something heavy hit him on the back of the head and he went down.

Raurí felt his strength drain away, weakness sweeping through him and making his movements sluggish. His attacker hit him again and he went face down, smelling earth and crushed vegetation. Waves of blackness and excruciating pain rendered him dizzy and sick. His attacker seeing him helpless moved on looking for another victim.

With an animal's instinct Raurí clawed at the earth, dragging himself deeper into the undergrowth, intuitively seeking to hide while wounded and vulnerable. His head was a solid mass of throbbing agony. It felt as if the back of his head was mashed to pulp. Wet and warm blood seeped down his neck and then he could move no more and a black pit opened and swallowed him, drowning out his pain and sickness.

CHAPTER TWENTY

When Raurí came too, he was face down in vegetation, the smell of crushed weeds and grasses strong in his nostrils, but stronger still was the agony in his head. He lay still while bands of pain washed over him, leaving him almost afraid to move in case the agony increased. Cautiously he lifted his head, closing his eyes as dizziness swept over him.

Raurí peered towards the chapel and could see lights inside. Fighting against the pain and dizziness, he crept close and peered through a fissure in the outer wall. He drew in a sharp breath. Sitting on the floor were his squad with their hands tied behind their backs. He also saw someone standing guard, armed with a machinegun. There was another figure in the shadows that Raurí couldn't make out. He heard movement behind him and dropped to the dirt. A bulky figure strode out of the shadows and went inside.

"What's happening?" someone asked and Raurí recognized the voice.

"Enda Moloney," he whispered, "so they got you as well."

"We can't find Mac Cathail."

Raurí rose up and peered inside, seeing immediately the bulky figure of Benedict Phelan and realizing that was the man who had just arrived. The person in the shadows stepped forward and Raurí recognized Enda Moloney.

"You got to find him," Moloney snarled. "He's the ringleader. If he escapes my life won't be worth a pint of buttermilk. I have to stay in the field. I'm close to naming the men who organize and run these raiding parties. The rebels trust me, for I have been feeding them information—nothing of any consequence. They think I'm their spy in Dublin Castle. If I'm caught then not only does it put my own life in danger but I won't be able to protect you."

"Don't worry," Phelan replied. "Mac Cathail won't get far."

"How the hell did you let him slip through the net? Get the hell out there and find him."

"Don't worry about Mac Cathail. I've sent men to watch for him at the creamery. Whichever way he goes we'll get him. What about this lot here?"

"We'll dispose of them in the usual way. They can join the other bodies out in the bog. But I must have Mac Cathail."

"Why is Mac Cathail so important?"

"It's unfinished business."

"What sort of unfinished business?"

"It's a family thing. His father discovered I was a spy with one foot in Dublin Castle and one foot in the Volunteers. I had to shut him up. Unfortunately his wife was with him at the time. I had no option but to kill them both. It looks like I need to complete the job and dispose of their brat as well. There's something about him that worries me. It's as if the ghost of his father had come back to haunt me."

Raurí slid to the ground, his brain reeling.

"Are you going to kill us?" a tremulous voice asked.

"Too right we are. But don't worry. It will be quick. A bullet in the back of the head. You won't even know it happened."

"You have to get us a priest. I don't want to die without the sacraments."

"You should have thought about that before coming here to steal our guns. But you'll not go away empty-handed. You'll take one bullet each with you."

"Time I was getting back," Moloney said.

"Yeah, I'll carry on the hunt for Mac Cathail," Phelan assured him.

Hidden in the shadows, Raurí watched the men emerge from the chapel.

"Don't worry about a thing, Enda. Mac Cathail's days are numbered. I thought I did for him once. He must have the luck of the devil to be still running around and causing all this trouble."

"Yeah, make sure you do it right this time. Whatever happens, keep me up to date."

When the men parted, each going their separate ways neither were aware of the shadowy figure that followed one of them.

Enda Moloney was not in a very good mood. Before he started out with the raiders he had made an excuse to go back to the house and phone Phelan so he could prepare an ambush. He shivered as he considered the coincidence that had brought the son of Pierce Mac Cathail into his life.

Moloney came to the small stream that had to be crossed to get to the meadow where he had left the donkeys. He had just stepped into the stream to wade across when there came a sudden movement behind and something landed on his back and he pitched forward into the water.

Raurí knelt on Moloney, his hands clasping the spy's head, keeping him submerged. A great rage had consumed him as he listened to the undercover agent confess to the murder of his parents and then callously condemn his men to death. That rage had transformed into a cold and deadly resolution.

As he held the man under, Raurí kept a watchful lookout in the surrounding night for any hint that he had been seen, and that men were coming to kill him as Moloney had instructed. Gradually the frantic struggles of the man in the stream lessened and ceased altogether, the last bubbles of air stopped coming to the surface. Raurí relaxed. Moloney the double agent would destroy no more lives. The murder of his parents had been avenged.

The guard inside the ancient chapel was leaning indolently against wall, holding his machine gun and smirking as he listened to the prisoners praying, taking pleasure in their distress.

"Don't worry, lads, next Sunday when I'm at Mass I'll light a candle for the repose of your souls," he called. "And when next I'm in O'Hegarty's bar, I'll raise a pint in memory of the brave men of Captain Mac Cathail's Brigade." He giggled. "Maybe I'll organize a collection to raise the money for a memorial plaque."

The sniggering guard caught a movement by the entrance. Belatedly he saw Raurí rushing towards him and raised his gun, his finger fumbling for the trigger. Raurí's hand gripped the scrabbling fingers in a powerful grip, brutally crushing the digits against the metal.

The man opened his mouth to scream and Raurí punched him hard in the face. His head jerked back against the wall. A glazed look came into the guard's eyes. Raurí punched again and the head bounced from the wall again. The man slid towards the floor. Such was Raurí's fury he kept punching as the man went down.

...RAURI PUNCHED HIM HARD IN THE FACE.

Raurí's punches burst open the man's lips and mashed his nose, blood spilling from the injuries. But the injuries to his face were as nothing compared to the terrible damage being done to the man's skull as with each brutal punch the back of his head cracked against the rough stones of the chapel wall. By the time he hit the floor the guard could feel no more pain nor would he be able to keep his promise to light a candle for his prisoners or raise a drink in their memory.

The prisoners had stopped their praying and were staring in amazement at the intruder. A babble of voices arose as men called out his name and tried to tell him what had happened. Raurí retrieved a knife from the body of the dead guard and set about cutting his men free. Sean Cassidy was the first to be freed and Raurí handed him the knife while he picked up the machinegun.

"I'll keep watch while you cut everybody free."

Raurí stepped to the entrance and peered out into the night. Cassidy came up behind him.

"We're ready, Raurí."

Raurí handed over the machine gun.

"Keep watch. You see anything move out there you cut loose with this. Don't hesitate. You lay down a curtain of fire and kill everything in sight."

He went back inside. The men were rubbing at chaffed wrists and massaging stiffened limbs, looking sheepishly at their captain.

"Was there any hint from Phelan's men where the guns were hidden?" Raurí asked

"When Phelan arrived he went over to that corner and then told Moloney nothing had been disturbed."

Raurí went across and held up the lamp. The light fell on an ancient tomb, the lid carved with Latin script. Raurí set down the lamp and pushed at the stone cover. Slowly the slab moved, grating across its housing, revealing steps leading to the interior.

"Boxes—all sorts of boxes," he observed. "Jerry, take a couple of men and bring the donkeys up to the chapel. Looks like we've found our weapons."

By the time the donkeys arrived the raiders had several boxes stacked outside the chapel. One box was broken open and the men armed themselves with rifles.

"We found Enda Moloney in the stream," Jerry said breathlessly. "Looks like the bastard drowned."

"Serves the treacherous bugger right. Fetch the body up and put him in the tomb. It'll be a nice little surprise for Phelan when he comes to collect his arms."

They lashed the boxes on the donkeys.

"Remember, don't be afraid to shoot anybody that challenges us," Raurí instructed his men. "We can't risk being captured. You've been sentenced to death once already tonight. Let that be a lesson to you. Shoot first and ask questions after."

They moved out, Raurí in the lead, his keen senses probing the night as they proceeded. Occasionally he would raise his hand and the little caravan would halt, waiting while he went ahead to check out the trail. At one point they had to stay quite still while the lights of an army lorry rumbled through on the nearby road, every man willing it not to stop. It droned on into the night, the headlights cutting a corridor in the darkness. They came to the gambling man's fairy ring and toiled up the steep slope. The donkeys were drooping as they were led inside the circle of trees, for the burdens they carried were heavy. The men were also wilting. Wearily the little band offloaded their haul.

"Leave your weapons here," Raurí ordered. "We need to get the donkeys back and then we're done. If there's any danger of being stopped we abandon the beasts and run for it."

They got the donkeys back to their home field without incident. Raurí had been thinking seriously about the situation as they made the journey and addressed his men before dismissing them.

"I can only say how proud I am of you. We had some reverses tonight during Operation Donkey Arms, the worst being the betrayal by that blackguard, Enda Moloney."

"Raurí, I have something to tell you," interrupted Gerry Morrison. "We heard some shocking things tonight at that place, but the most terrible news of all was about your mother and father."

There came a murmuring of voices and a shuffling of feet as the volunteers grew uncomfortable with the knowledge of what Morrison was about to tell Raurí.

"What about them?"

Raurí wanted no one to know he had killed Moloney. He preferred them to believe the spy had accidentally drowned.

"Moloney said he killed your dad because he found out he was a spy for Dublin Castle."

Raurí stood for a long time without speaking; making believe the impact of this piece of information had stunned him into silence.

"My father murdered. I always thought my parents drowned at sea," he said eventually.

"I'm sorry, Raurí to tell you this but I thought you ought to know."

"You were right to tell me. And now Moloney the murderer has drowned. Maybe there is some sort of primitive justice at work here. Thank you, Jerry. Back to tonight. Phelan knows us all now. My guess is he'll come after us, or he might inform the RIC. The former is the more likely for he'll want those guns back. We might have to go on the run until this dies down or we go after Phelan ourselves.

"Go home and make whatever preparations you need to go into hiding for a time. If Phelan's men take you they'll torture you to make you tell where the arms are hidden and then kill you."

The volunteers dispersed. Raurí watched them depart then set out himself. He was almost staggering with exhaustion. It had been a long and fraught-filled night. He had no idea of the time but guessed it could not be much before dawn.

His head was throbbing. During the rescue of his men he had tried to ignore the pain, but now it nagged him. He wanted nothing more than to sink into his bed and sleep for a week. But he knew that was not possible. There was still much to do.

Had he not been so tired and had his head not been so sore he might have noticed the bulky figure on the side of the road. As it was he was taken by surprise as someone crashed into him and tumbled him into the roadside ditch.

CHAPTER TWENTY-ONE

Raurí struggled against the weight of the man pinning him down, but the ordeals he'd had to endure in the course of the night had weakened him and he could make no headway against his attacker.

"Lie still you eejit."

"Damian! What the hell are you doing?"

The weight eased off and his friend crouched beside him.

"There are fellas skulking around the place so I came out to wait for you to save you blundering into them."

"Yeah, they're probably Phelan's men. Whereabouts are they?"

"Down the road near that big clump of bushes."

"Right, here's the plan. Wander up the road there and pretend to be drunk."

Damian sauntered along singing in a rambling drunken manner. Concealing himself in the ditch Raurí crept after the singer. Damian had just passed the hidden watchers when he paused and raised his arms in the air. He then spoke in sculptural tones.

"Now is the winter of our discontent..."

Raurí smiled wryly as he heard his friend reciting the opening lines of Shakespeare's Richard III. He got the smell of tobacco and stale sweat coming off the men as he neared their hiding place. Raurí was tempted to shoot the men down without warning, for he was aware of Phelan's sentence of death upon him, but he could not bring himself to do so. The men watching his house were guilty only of following orders. Raurí crouched low so he would not make a target, for he knew the watchers would be armed.

"All right you men; I have a gun on you. Put your hands above your head and step out on the road."

Had they been sensible, the men would have done what they were told. As it was they swivelled towards the source of the voice and Raurí heard the distinct click of rifle bolts. Gun flashes jetted into the night as the men fired. Bullets whistled overhead and out into the night.

The men were no more than fifteen to twenty yards away and Raurí emptied his revolver at the rifle flashes. The trigger clicked on empty and Raurí flattened in the dirt ejecting the spent cases. The small rattles as he did so seemingly loud in the sudden silence.

"Raurí," Damian called. "I think they're done for."

Raurí finished reloading and walked towards the downed men.

"They're both dead," Damian said. "Couldn't you have held your fire until I finished my performance?"

"It was so awful I saved one bullet for you if you were still reciting. Maybe I shouldn't have bothered shooting them. They would have died of boredom in any case."

"You're a bloody philistine, Raurí Mac Cathail."

Raurí was staring soberly at the dead men.

"What are we going to do with these boogers?" He nudged one of the rifles with his foot. "At least we got two good rifles out of it."

"Raurí, we'll have to get the bodies away from the creamery. If the police find them anywhere near here they'll make that an excuse to arrest you and wreck the creamery into the bargain."

"You're right. We'll fetch the cart out and dump them well away from here. But if we're caught they'll hang us for sure."

Just then the idea of transporting the bodies became a nonstarter, for out in the night they heard the faint hum of an engine. The plotters stared at each other in consternation.

"We'll have to make a run for it," Damian said.

"Wait." Raurí bent down and picked up a rifle. "You get the hell out of here. I have an idea that just might work."

"What are you going to do?"

"You get as far away as possible. Go back home."

Raurí was watching the headlights in the distance.

"Raurí," Damian's hand was on Raurí tugging at him. "Come with me."

"Damian, do as you're told. That's an order."

Reluctantly Damian slouched off, frequently turning his head and seeing Raurí standing in the road with the rifle. Raurí watched the lorry rolling towards him, its headlights illuminating the road as it progressed. He raised his weapon and cuddled it into his shoulder, training the sights above the headlights. Slowly he took up the pressure on the trigger. And so he waited, while the lorry, full of soldiers ground towards him.

"Steady," Raurí said, "nerves of steel are what are needed now."

The headlights coming closer and closer—brighter and brighter—lighting up the road.

"Steady," Raurí spoke again as he squinted along the barrel of his rifle. "Any time now."

His finger took up the slack in the trigger—the headlights blinding, as the lorry rushed towards him. Raurí squeezed the trigger, the repercussion kicking into his shoulder. But he was prepared for that.

He fired again and again and the lorry swerved to one side of the road and then veered back again. A bullet from Raurí's rifle smashed the driver's shoulder and he was struggling to hold on to the steering wheel. As the windscreen shattered the officer beside him fumbled for his revolver. The soldiers in the back of the lorry were yelling and cursing as they were thrown about by the erratic performance of their transport.

The magazine empty, Raurí tossed the rifle on top the body of the man who had owned the weapon. He turned and fled. Behind him the driver lost control and the lorry crashed into the ditch throwing him through the shattered windscreen. The headlights were still shining, illuminating the bottom of the roadside ditch.

In the back of the lorry there was chaos as the soldiers were tossed in a tangle, swearing and yelling. The captain, bruised and shaken, kept enough of his wits about him to raise his revolver and fire through the broken windscreen. He got off several shots where he thought the ambusher had gone to ground. Then he tumbled to the road calling out to his men.

"Everyone out. Weapons at the ready."

He was reloading his revolver and looking for a target. He fired another volley to where he had last seen the rifleman. Behind him his men tumbled from the back of the wagon. Fumbling with their weapons the soldiers lined up across the road.

"By those bushes there," the officer roared. "Fire. That's where the blighters are."

A fusillade of shots tore into the night. Bullets flayed the foliage, smashing twigs and branches to shreds. Some ricocheted from the road but most sped off into the night. Getting to his feet the officer waved his men forward.

"Half of you come with me. The rest cover us. If you have a firm target do not hesitate to fire. And someone see to Private Monks. He was thrown through the windscreen."

The soldiers advanced down the road, weapons at the ready, stopping by the clump of bushes where the rifleman was last seen. Cautiously the officer peered into the ditch. In the gloom he could see two bodies. Lying beside them were a couple of rifles. Slowly the tension went out of him.

"By Jove, I believe we've put those blackguards out of action. Jackson, climb down there and see if those bastards are still alive."

It took only a short examination to discover the men in the ditch were very dead. The officer holstered his weapon.

"Watson and Gilbert, I want you to stand guard over these bodies. The rest of you spread out along the road. But stay alert; there might be more of the murdering bastards lurking around. I'll go back and see what the damage has been done to the vehicle and find out how Monks is. Poor blighter took a bullet and then was thrown through the windscreen."

Half an hour later the patrol arrived at the creamery, the nearest building to the ambush site. After hammering on the door and shouting, it was eventually opened by Raurí, yawning widely.

"What's the bloody racket?" he grumbled, as he eyed the squad of soldiers in the yard. "Don't you know what time of the night it is?"

"We got a wounded man here," the officer told him. "He needs urgent medical attention. Where's the nearest doctor?"

The request galvanized Raurí.

"Bring him in here. What happened?"

"We were ambushed back down the road. Didn't you hear the shots?

Quite a gun battle it was. There were two of them firing at us. Hit the lorry and it's in the ditch now."

"Holy, Mary and Joseph! I never heard a thing. I was sleeping sound."

Raurí rooted around and come up with bandages and cotton pads. One of the soldiers took it on himself to tend his wounded comrade.

"I'll get some water on the boil. Maybe you men would like a brew."

"That's dammed decent of you. What's your name? I'm Captain Trent."

"Raurí Mac Cathail, sir. Maybe you want to use the telephone; let your HQ know what's happened."

"Splendid."

Raurí showed Captain Travis the telephone and spent the next ten minutes making mugs of tea and serving it up to the grateful soldiers.

"Thank you, sir."

"Very kind of you, sir."

"Bless you, sir."

Raurí was full of curiosity about the action that had taken place several hundred yards from his home while he slept through it all.

"And you got the boogers?" he asked.

"Riddled them! Full of holes they are. If they took a drink of this here tea, it'd sprinkle all back out again."

The next few hours were hectic as more soldiers descended on the creamery and Raurí spent most of that time catering to the needs of a few dozen soldiers, making tea and handing out slabs of cheese and biscuits, which was devoured with much relish. Eventually Captain Trent gave the order for the soldiers to get back in the lorries. Before he left he came up to Raurí and shook his hand.

"Mr Mac Cathail, I am most grateful for all you have done for us. It's as I have been trying to tell my superiors. Not all Irishmen are rebels. Some of you are quite decent chaps."

Raurí stood at the door of his home and waved to his departing enemies.

"Goodbye, do call again."

He came inside; lay down on the settee with the intention of planning his next move, but instead fell asleep.

CHAPTER TWENTY-TWO

When Raurí awoke, Ivor had returned from Dublin. His uncle told them there was no money or guns to be had from the army council.

"Your worries are over, uncle," Raurí said, and told Ivor about his night-time escapade.

Ivor was all business once he knew of the existence of the arms cache.

"We'll have to move it. I know the very place. Harness up the wagon."

Ivor, along with Raurí, transported the arms to a small cave inside a Tor.

"This way if Phelan does take one of your men and squeeze the information out of him it won't do him any good," Ivor observed.

Leaving Raurí at the cave the older man drove the empty wagon back home. Raurí broke open boxes and sorted through the weapons and ammunition.

'We have enough here to arm the whole republican army,' he mused.

Raurí camouflaged the entrance to the cave with ferns and branches before setting off home. As he jogged back he felt the influence of the wolf surging through him but suppressed the urge to change. It would be madness to initiate a transformation during daylight hours. A wolf streaking across the countryside would spark off a panic and initiate a hunt for the beast.

Night was his time and when it was safe to give in to his urges and run wild and free and preferably in the company of Aishling. As if the thought had summoned her, he was suddenly aware of her on the road ahead.

"Raurí I came to warn you," she called as they neared. "There's a police tender up at the house."

"The peelers! I'll wait for them to leave before heading down."

He pulled her to the side of the road and they pushed through a gap in the hedge into a meadow; a colourful mixture of wild flowers. Slowly, in passionate embrace, they sank to the ground, the scent of flowers a heady mixture adding to their sense of need. Raurí held her face in both his hands and gazed longingly into Aishling's eyes heavy with want.

She was wearing a polka dot cotton dress that clung to her figure. In the tumble to the ground it had ridden up over her thighs exposing muscular tanned legs. Lost in the immense pleasure of mutual affection the world around them disappeared. Suddenly their pleasure was interrupted by the sounds of gunfire. Suddenly the real world came crashing back.

"Oh my god! What's happening?"

Raurí was on his feet starting towards the noise.

"Careful, Raurí, Don't go rushing back there."

"I got to have a look. I just have to."

As they came within sight of the house, the police tender was still parked in the yard. They sidled into the shelter of the hedge. As the youngsters crept closer, they could hear shouting. The commotion grew louder as the policemen exited the buildings. There came the roar of an engine and the lorry drove out of the yard.

There was an ominous silence as they approached the creamery. Raurí's feeling of dread grew at the sight of blood on the threshold. With deep foreboding he entered the house stopping short as he saw the devastation.

The large dresser that stood against the wall for as long as Raurí could remember had been pushed over and now lay face down. Shards of crockery were scattered over the floor, swimming in spilled milk. The table had been overturned and someone had battered it with the chairs, splintering the legs and backs.

"Uncle Ivor."

There was no reply. Slowly Raurí stepped further into the room, broken crockery crunching beneath his boots.

"Uncle Ivor."

There was still no reply.

"Take a look around. You go upstairs and I'll go out back."

Raurí made his way through the house, a pit of fear growing in his stomach. There was no sign of his uncle but every room had been trashed. Aishling was shaking her head as she appeared in the doorway.

"The place is a complete mess. The pictures even smashed on the walls. They just went on a wrecking spree."

Raurí turned and walked towards the byre. The strong smell of cordite and blood hit him like a physical force. He stopped, unwilling to go any further; afraid of what he would find. Aishling moved beside him and took his hand in hers.

It took a great effort for Raurí to step inside and then he stopped, gave a low moan and fell back against the lintel. He rushed back outside, breathing heavily, trying not to be sick. It took all his courage to go back inside.

The byre was a bloodbath. Cows lay in their stalls in pools of their own blood. All had been riddled with bullets. Hanging on to his sanity and his bile, Raurí walked along the row of stalls. Aishling stayed by the doorway.

The cows lay in grotesque attitudes of death. Some had tried to jump out of the stalls and had been shot hanging over gates, blood still dripping on the straw that had been their bedding. Most lay in their enclosures, shot at close range. The killers had walked along pouring bullets into the defenceless animals. The place stank of death and blood and shit, where animals had fouled as the killers worked their way along the stalls. Raurí heard a groan. Quickly he moved towards the sound. In the corner of the byre someone was lying in the straw.

"Damian!" Raurí was immediately down on his knees beside his friend. "My god, Damian."

Across Damian's forehead was a deep gash from which blood flowed freely. He screwed up his eyes to peer at Raurí, blinking to clear his vision.

"I tried to stop them. The poor cows... why would they do that, Raurí? They were like crazy men laughing and shooting. I thought they would shoot me."

His voice faded and he stared vacantly into space.

"Let's get you up to the house."

With Aishling helping, he got Damian to his feet and they helped him up to the house. When he had Damian resting on the settee, the covering ripped with the stuffing partly pulled out, Raurí searched for something to attend his friend's cuts.

"Get hot water," Aishling told him, "and make a pot of tea if there is anything left unbroken. I'll take care of Damian."

"Where's Uncle Ivor?" Raurí asked, when he returned with the basin of water.

"They took him."

Raurí stared at Damian.

"Why would they do that?"

"They said they had a tipoff he was hoarding arms and wanted to know where they were. Ivor told them he was an ex-soldier and had sworn an oath to the king. Two of the peelers held him while Maguire hit him. Towards the end Ivor could hardly talk. His face was a bloody mess. He just kept muttering, 'I'm a loyal subject'. The others were searching through the house wrecking whatever they could get their hands on. Maguire said if Ivor didn't tell him where the guns were they would shoot the cows. It was terrible, Raurí, terrible."

Damian lapsed into silence. Aishling washed and tended his injuries. Raurí searched the wreckage finding a saucepan and some tin mugs, his thoughts filled with foreboding as he contemplated his uncle's fate at the hands of the police.

"Someone betrayed us. It's someone in our brigade. We need to find out who it was and deal with them. But first we have to get Ivor back from the peelers."

"Get Ivor back! How we going to do that? And what about the cows—what are we to do?"

"I'll call in on Tully's knacker's yard. Tell him what's happened. He'll know what to do. You stay here and help him if you're up to it."

"What will you be doing?"

Raurí stared at Damian who shivered as he saw the look in his friend's eyes.

"Me—I'll be rounding up some of the boys. Then I'm going to the barracks and ask Sergeant Maguire to release Uncle Ivor."

CHAPTER TWENTY-THREE

A bridge spanned the River Tuam and it was this police vehicles traversed when leaving their barracks. Underneath the wide arches of the bridge the members of Raurí's brigade hid while they waited for the evening patrol to leave. Further up the road, Aishling lay out of sight watching for traffic. Her instructions were to alert the brigade to any activity on the road that might indicate reinforcements approaching the barracks. The men were tense as they waited; Raurí having imposed an order for strict silence.

Raurí was somewhat uneasy, for one of his men had gone missing. His uncle had promoted McCrudden to sergeant and Raurí worried that he had been taken by the security forces and even now was being pressured to expose their plans.

He questioned his men but no one knew anything about the absent sergeant. It was a loose end that nagged at Raurí. And then he had more urgent things to worry about as the roar of a lorry was heard approaching the bridge. At that moment someone farted loud enough to be heard above the noise of the engine.

Even Raurí, tense and worried about the outcome of the raid, could not repress his amusement as mirth swept over the men beneath the bridge. It might have been nervous laughter but at least it released some of the tension within the group.

"Dunlop, save that until we get inside the barracks. We won't have to fire a shot if you release enough of that."

"He's a one-man arsenal. The British could have used him in France against the Germans."

"Yeah, I'd rather a dose of mustard gas than one of Dunlop's farts."

"All right, men," Raurí called them to order. "Remember—keep out of sight while I'm walking up to the gate. As soon as I've overpowered the guard, you come up to join me. And make it quick. I don't want to be holding off the whole damn barracks while you lot dawdle about. Once we're inside we'll secure the building and rescue Major Foyle. Disarm any peelers and take them outside. Then we set the place on fire. The grenades should do the trick. With any luck we'll be long gone before the patrol returns. Any questions? "

No one spoke and Raurí climbed up on the bridge and walked towards the barracks—an ugly stone building standing squat and menacing above the town, dominating and cowing its citizens. As he advanced, Raurí felt naked and vulnerable. He put his hand on the butt of the revolver inside his jacket to reassure himself he had the means to defend himself should something go amiss.

"Hello, hello, open up, please. Hello!"

Raurí hammered on the wicket door in the large wooden gateway. A small trapdoor slid open and a face peered out.

"What the hell do you want?"

"I've been told Ivor Foyle is being held here. I need to find out what's happening."

"What's your name?"

"Raurí Mac Cathail, I'm Ivor Foyle's nephew. I was told he was arrested this morning. I need find out what this is about."

With a thud the trapdoor slid shut. Raurí could hear bolts being withdrawn and waited while the door was opened.

"You'd better come inside."

Raurí did as he was bid and stepped into the yard, his hand gripping his revolver, ready to pull it and take the policeman prisoner.

"Wait here while I go and fetch someone."

The policeman turned and marched across the stone-flagged yard, leaving Raurí alone at the gate.

"Jeez, how easy was that."

Raurí waited until the uniformed figure disappeared through a door at the other side of the yard, then turned and undid the postern gate. He leaned out and made frantic signals. Seeing his men approaching, Raurí stepped back inside, drew his revolver and stood watching the yard. One by one the squad stepped inside. As the last man came through, a bright light lit up the sky. The raiding party glanced up at the arcing tracer. They stared uncomprehendingly at the artificial light in the night sky, painting the yard and the raider's pale faces with a ghostly luminance.

"A flare, what does that mean?"

• • •

Aishling watched the flare from her hiding place. She realized the barracks was sending out a distress signal. What puzzled her was the lack of gunfire. Surely if there was fighting there would be shooting but there was nothing. Somewhere in the distance a noise was growing. Aishling immediately guessed what it was. The police tender was returning—probably in response to the signal flare. She had to warn Raurí.

Aishling quickly ran towards the barracks. As she approached the bridge she heard the tramp of marching feet and crouched down—a dark shape among the shadows.

From the direction of the town came a body of men tramping towards the bridge as only disciplined and trained men do. With mounting dread she watched the column approach the bridge until they were close enough for her to discern more details. They were, as she had surmised, a body of policemen marching to the barracks.

Behind her the noise of the lorry was getting louder. Aishling realized she would not be in time to warn Raurí. The odds against the squad surviving the night were getting slimmer and slimmer. Desperate times needed desperate actions. Aishling quickly unlimbered her revolver and taking aim at the squad of marching policemen loosed of a volley of shots at them.

• • •

Inside the yard Raurí was barking orders.

"Take shelter!" he roared "Kick down the doors and get inside before they start shooting."

Strangely no shots were coming as yet, which gave Raurí hope they could get inside some of the buildings and fight from sheltered positions. As his men battered at the stout wooden doors Raurí heard a noise from above his head. He was instantly alert scanning the upper floors. A window opened and Raurí aimed his revolver upwards.

A man's unshod feet appeared across the sill. Raurí watched puzzled as a pair of bare legs followed after the feet. Slowly the rest of the figure was revealed until a naked man could be seen sitting in the window, his feet dangling.

Raurí stared at this apparition. Then he noticed the noose around the neck of the seated figure. His men followed his gaze, staring up at the strange sight. The features were distorted and swollen into a bizarre caricature of a man's face but even so Raurí recognized him.

"Uncle Ivor."

The men in the yard had ceased their efforts to break inside and were staring horrified at the naked figure of the major. Suddenly rifle barrels appeared at windows. Raurí's men dropped into firing positions in the stone courtyard but no shots as yet were fired.

"Drop your weapons at once or Foyle dies." The voice boomed into the yard magnified by a hailer. "If you don't drop your weapons you will all die."

Raurí could not take his eyes off the naked figure seated on the window.

"Uncle Ivor," he whimpered helplessly.

"I'm counting to ten and if you have not disarmed by then, we start shooting. We have enough firepower to annihilate you. I'm counting now—one."

The naked man was shaking his head and mouthing something through swollen, bloodied lips.

"Two."

"Raurí, what are we to do?"

"Three. Remember Foyle dies first."

"Four."

"Raurí, for God's sake say something."

"Five. Remember you'll all die in that yard."

"Six. What'll it be gentlemen: death or glory?"

"Seven."

Raurí watched in despair as his uncle kept shaking his head and making awkward movements with his ruined lips, the distorted sounds never quite reaching him. It was obvious what he was trying to tell Raurí. No Surrender! And Raurí's anguish grew as he contemplated what he had to do.

"Eight. Start saying your prayers, rebels for tonight you die."

From outside the barracks came the sound of shots.

● ● ●

Aishling's shots brought down the leading policemen, sowing confusion among the rest of the group. The unexpected ambush on the bridge immediately created mayhem as the column of police dived for cover; some throwing themselves onto the road while others jumped over the parapet.

She raced back up the road, careless of being seen. The firing would alert the raiders that something was amiss. If she hindered the policemen sufficiently it might give Rauri's squad enough time to extricate themselves from the barracks and make their escape. Aishling knew Rauri's situation would be dire and what she was doing could only hope to delay the reinforcements.

The headlights of the lorry could be seen in the distance as it roared back to support their comrades. Aishling stopped her headlong rush and went to cover at the side of the road. She reloaded and crouched in the ditch waiting for the oncoming vehicle.

When she judged the moment right, Aishling stood upright, grasped her revolver in both hands and fired steadily at the approaching headlights. The lorry swerved to one side but righted again and the driver accelerated towards her.

Aishling emptied her revolver, the shots blasting out one of the headlights—the last shots almost point blank. The policemen in the lorry were shooting back. Bullets whistled overhead and around her but then the lorry swept past and her revolver was empty. Aishling watched in despair as the lorry raced on, knowing they would join with the group at the bridge and together form a formidable force that must overwhelm Rauri's squad.

The lorry was going faster and faster and then disaster struck as it hurtled into the bend in the road. There was a screech of brakes and the squealing of tyres and the lorry spun out of control. A wheel went in the ditch and the vehicle lurched as the driver tried to pull it back but it was too late and the back end swung around. The rear wheels dropped off the road. For a moment the whole thing tottered, off-balance. And then it toppled over. The roar of the engine faded and stopped. As the motor died it was replaced by the cries of injured men.

Aishling watched with grim satisfaction the chaos she had caused. She could do no more for Rauri's raiders. Hopefully her delaying tactics had given them time to get out from the barracks.

• • •

"Nine. At the count of ten we open fire."

The sound of firing from outside the barracks convinced Raurí reinforcements were being brought up.

"Enough, I surrender." Raurí tossed down his gun and raised his hands. "Throw down your weapons, men. They have us cold."

It was hopeless. They would be cut to ribbons should they decide to fight. Once the shooting started, Raurí doubted if any of the men in the courtyard would survive. They were well and truly trapped.

"Step away from the weapons and line up against the wall," the disembodied voice ordered.

Despondently his men shuffled back, hands elevated. Suddenly the yard was full of armed police officers. Raurí gazed up at his uncle still poised naked on the window ledge.

"I'm sorry, Uncle Ivor," he called, not knowing if he could hear.

Raurí turned his attention back to the policemen now covering them with rifles and some armed with submachine guns. In the face of all this firepower he knew his decision to surrender was the right one. Trapped in the courtyard they wouldn't have stood a chance. At last Sergeant Maguire appeared. The sergeant was big and brutal looking and running to fat. The peeler brandished a revolver as he approached the prisoners.

"Someone gather up these weapons. Can't leave them there as a temptation to these murdering rebels."

Constables scuttled forward to collect the guns. As they did so from outside there came more shots. Maguire grinned.

"Sounds as if your rearguard is being wiped out," the big sergeant said. "How many more of you are there?"

"Don't you know?" Raurí answered bitterly. "You seem to know all about us. Who ratted on us? And for God's sake have some respect for Major Foyle. Take him inside and let him get some clothes on."

There was movement from one of the doorways and another figure stepped out. Raurí's heart sank as he recognized the man.

"Mac Cathail," Benedict Phelan crowed, "well and truly trapped."

"Phelan, you are a traitor to your people," Raurí said bitterly. "While Irish men and women are fighting and dying to free their country you are like a fat leech battening on our misery."

Phelan cursed and launched himself at Raurí. The youngster reacted swiftly as the bigger man came at him. He sprang forward and using his head as a battering ram cannoned into Phelan catching him in the guts. There was a whoosh of expelled breath and Phelan staggered back. Raurí

"ENOUGH, I SURRENDER."

kept after him pummelling the big man with brutal punches. They both went down with R_auri_ on top. He kept on punching. The big man was bellowing like a downed heifer.

"Get him off me. Get him away from me."

But none of the policemen came to help. Some might even have moved a few paces to get a better view of the fight. Then a figure darted forward. Raurí saw the movement and turned from his frenzied attack to meet the new challenge. Momentarily he stopped and gaped at the newcomer. McCrudden—his missing sergeant!

He had a rifle in his hands and was swinging it at Raurí. Too late he tried to duck and the rifle caught him on the side of the head. Raurí just had time to curse out loud as he realized who had betrayed him before stars exploded in his head and he tumbled from atop Phelan. Raurí tried to roll away. McCrudden was on him swinging with the rifle once more.

"Malachi why...?" Raurí wanted to ask, but the barrack yard was spinning around.

He tried to focus but the rifle barrel crunched on top of his head and he sank down into a vortex of pain and blackness.

CHAPTER TWENTY-FOUR

As the murkiness cleared from Raurí's head it ushered in waves of pain. He opened his eyes and throbbing agony pierced his brain as he tried to focus. Slowly his vision cleared. He was looking out across a yard crowded with armed police. Raurí tried to move and discovered his arms were stretched out each side of him. Slowly painfully he turned his head and stared at the rope fastening his wrist to iron rings on the wall. He gazed at his naked limbs realizing the policemen had stripped him.

"Ah, I see you are back with us."

Raurí focused on Sergeant Maguire's coarse sneering face.

"I didn't want you to miss any of the highlights of the evening. We are laying on some entertainment for you."

Raurí gazed at the police officer, not answering. He turned his head to see his squad lined up alongside him, stripped naked and arms and wrists bound as he was to the walls.

"Do what you want with me, but let these men go. I told them we were coming here to rescue you from an attack we heard was due to be made on the barrack. They are your friends, not your enemies."

Maguire threw back his head and laughed.

"Aw, Captain Mac Cathail, you do spin a wild yarn."

Phelan loomed up beside the police sergeant.

"He is an entertaining booger, Sergeant, but don't be fooled. He's a slippery swine. Twice I had him dead to rights and twice he eluded me."

Phelan reached out and backhanded Raurí across the face. Raurí's head rocked from the blow and new waves of agony swept through him.

"One night we beat the bejeezus out of him. We were sure he was dead when we threw him in the ditch. No ordinary man could have survived. A few weeks later he's walking around bold as brass.

"Another night we laid an ambush for him and his crew and the booger escaped again. He has a charmed life. So make sure when it's time to finish him you do it properly. My advice is to drive a wooden stake in his heart to make sure he stays dead. There's something uncanny the way he keeps cheating death."

Raurí was blinking away tears of pain. Phelan! Always it came back to Phelan. A veil parted in his head and it was then he recalled the night of the *ceilidh* and the gang that waylaid him on his way home. The memory of it came flooding back.

It was Phelan who had beaten him senseless that night. It was because of Phelan he had become half-man, half-beast. Raurí glared with hatred at the smuggler and knew somehow he had to revenge himself on the thug.

"Oh don't worry, Benedict," Maguire answered. "He'll die all right. But he'll have to suffer before we allow him the luxury of death. By the time we have finished with him he'll be begging us to finish him."

The sergeant turned and raised his arm, pointing upward. Raurí arched his neck to peer up and caught his breath. Ivor's naked form was still sitting in the window, slumped forward—held from toppling into the yard by a leather strap which passed under his arms and around his chest.

"You evil bastards!" he croaked. "Let him go. He's done nothing wrong. He's a bloody hero. He fought in Africa for your English overlords and was decorated for bravery. He's worth more than this whole barrack of peelers."

The youngster strained at his bonds but even with his great strength he could not break the ropes.

"He does carry on like a raging animal. And come to think on it he is bloody hairy. Like a goddamn gorilla. You want your uncle released? Tell us where you hid the guns and then we'll let him go."

Raurí stared balefully at the sergeant, forcing back his anger.

"You'll release him?"

"I said I would. Don't you trust the word of a policeman?"

And Raurí remembered the big police sergeant back in Dublin. Sergeant Delaney had been an evil, treacherous creature and now Raurí had to deal with another one cut from the same cloth.

"Swear it to me. Swear you'll let him go."

"Raurí, my boy, would I lie to you? I give you my word. You cough up those weapons and we'll let your uncle go."

"All right then. You release him and I'll tell you, or better still I'll take you there."

"Not so fast my canny friend. We need some proof of your good faith. It is all right you asking me to make a promise, but I need your promise also."

Raurí looked up at the naked form balanced on the window ledge. Ivor slumped forward. Blood encrusted his swollen features.

"Why have you got that rope around his neck?"

"He was sentenced to hang for murder and treason. We've stayed the execution out of compassion. Also I wanted you to be present when he hanged so you can witness for yourself the penalty for defying the legitimate forces of law and order."

"You call this law and order," Raurí replied bitterly. "It's lynch law."

The sergeant reached out and grasped the naked youngster beneath the chin forcing his head back, at the same time choking him.

"Tell me where those arms are, or Foyle dies now."

Raurí gasped and struggled against the sergeant's grip, but he was helpless. The fingers squeezed tighter. Raurí's eyes watered and he twisted feebly like a rabbit in the grip of a fox. He saw the killer impulse in the policeman's eyes and knew he was near death and he almost welcomed it.

It would be one way of escaping the tough choices facing him. He had to return those hard-won weapons, or watch his uncle die on the end of a rope. He knew there was no other choice. As the choke hold on his neck tightened he could feel his senses reeling. He opened his mouth wide in an effort to suck in air. Abruptly Maguire released his grip and stepped back.

"Do you want the deaths of these men on your conscience?"

"No, no..." Raurí gasped, trying to get his voice working again. "I'll tell you where the arms are. Slieve Garret—I hid them in a cave."

Maguire turned to Phelan.

"What do you think? Is he telling the truth?"

"Hard to tell, he's a slimy git."

"Wait, I think he's telling the truth."

McCrudden, Raurí's double-crossing sergeant, stepped forward.

"When I followed him and Foyle, they went up there, but I couldn't get any further without being spotted. I think he's telling it right."

"Treacherous bastard," Raurí growled.

Helpless and impotent, he imagined being free and in his alter being, attacking the foul trio. It would give him great pleasure to rip and slash these brutes and leave them sprawling in the courtyard covered in their own gore. But that was wishful thinking. He was fastened securely with sturdy ropes. His enemies had the upper hand and he could only bide his time and hope for an opportunity to escape.

"Very good." Maguire turned to Phelan. "Take your men and recover the arms. And next time don't be so careless. I can't always guarantee to pull your ass out of the fire."

"I want to hang around and watch Mac Cathail get his punishment," Phelan replied. "This time I want to make sure the bastard is dead and won't come back to cause any more trouble."

"Don't worry. His end won't be quick. I have a special treatment laid on for young Raurí Mac Cathail. In fact before you leave to recover your arms I will give you a foretaste of what lies in store for him."

As he finished speaking Maguire stepped forward until he was directly in front of Raurí.

"I said I would let your uncle go if you collaborated with us."

Raurí stared back at the policeman and his foreboding grew as he saw the malicious gleam in the man's eyes. He said nothing, waiting, wondering what the brute was up to. Maguire turned and made a signal towards the window where Raurí's uncle slumped naked and bloody.

"Finn, let the booger go."

And Raurí guessed what was about to happen. His uncle's body leaned out from the window. Raurí saw the strap that held him in place pulled away.

"Nooo...."

The naked man leaned forward, tipping further and further.

"No, please no!"

But there was no stopping that inexorable movement as the naked man, shorn of all dignity, toppled from his perch and fell out into space. He did not fall far. Abruptly his fall was halted as the rope around his neck wrenched him to an abrupt stop.

Raurí watched in horror as his Uncle Ivor jerked and kicked on the end of the rope. He could see his ruined mouth opening wide as he gasped for air. But the noose was biting into his neck, and the strangulation was prolonged as the hanging man drove his heels into the stone wall in an effort to push up against the pressure on his neck. The face was mottled as the choking man struggled. Raurí could watch no more. He dropped his head and wept as he gave in to despair. Sergeant Maguire saw Raurí's head droop and moved swiftly. Brutally he gripped him by the hair and jerked his head back.

"Watch, you bastard! That's what happens to all rebels."

There were tears in Raurí's eyes, partially distorting his vision as he was forced to witness the death throes of his beloved uncle. He had to watch as the struggles grew weaker and weaker. And then it was over. Ivor Foyle, one time sergeant major in the British army, and lately a major in the Irish Republican Army, hung naked and bloody from a rope, while his nephew sobbed helplessly in the yard below him.

"Go and recover the arms, Phelan. That was only the opening act. There's a lot more to come. We'll make these rebels suffer before we send them all to hell. They'll learn that no one messes with the Royal Irish Constabulary."

CHAPTER TWENTY-FIVE

Once Phelan and his men had left on their mission, Maguire sent into town for supplies. The police tender returned loaded with crates of Guinness. As the night advanced the revelry got fully underway.

Along with the porter there were demijohns of pocheen, a potent, illegal spirit that was brewed in isolated bogs or lonely woodlands. The sounds of revelry echoed out from the barracks.

Raurí, and his captured squad, were left to suffer, hanging naked and shivering in their bonds, while the police garrison celebrated the capture of the IRA brigade and the hanging of its leader.

There was no one on guard. Everyone was inside drinking and carousing. There was no need for a watch. The people who might have given trouble were safe in the courtyard; secured to iron rings that had been used as hitching rings at a time when the force used horses as their means of transport. The lifeless figure of Ivor was left dangling as a reminder to the captured rebels of the fate that awaited them.

Raurí drooped in his bonds, occasionally straightening up as he tried to ease the discomfort of the ropes binding him to the wall. He had struggled in vain to wrench himself free. All he had achieved were raw wrists as the rough rope chaffed his skin.

He raised his head and looked across at his fellow captives. Like him, they sagged listlessly, all hope of reprieve drained away. The lynching of their much loved and respected major had knocked all ideas of resistance from their thoughts. They hung listlessly from their restraints, given to despair.

Raurí thought about Aishling and wondered if she was safe. He had heard the gunfire earlier and realized she must have run into trouble. He took comfort from the fact that his captors had not produced her as he was sure they would have done if she had been captured or killed. His contemplation of Aishling reminded him of their unique relationship and the secret life they shared.

Wolf-man and wolf-woman, they were bound together by their un-conventional existence; half-human half-beast. He recalled their carefree frolicking both in human and in animal form and now as his life was about to end, he realized he loved the wildness and beauty of the woman who had helped save his life.

"I love you, Aishling," he murmured through blood-encrusted and swollen lips.

Raurí regretted he had never said those words to her. He pictured her again as a lovely young woman and also as a splendid wolf. As he slipped in and out of consciousness these thoughts became dominant in his mind and he imagined he was free to run wild and to cavort once more with his beloved.

In this half-dreaming state he was doing something he had not thought practical in his present situation. In a reverie he saw himself again in his other state and reality overcame him and he started the change. With a shock he realized what was happening as his body went through its painful metamorphism.

Raurí tried to reverse the transformation but he was too far gone and had to endure the agony as his body adapted to his beast-form while awkwardly pinned to the wall. Guiltily he glanced around to see if anyone noticed his transformation.

But there was no one to witness the change from man to wolf. His fellow prisoners were too wrapped up in their own misery to notice anything but their own hopeless state. And the police were busily getting gloriously drunk within the warmth and shelter of the barracks.

In the gloom of the courtyard, the great black beast strained at the bonds that bit cruelly into the flesh of his limbs. It was to no avail. The beast had no more success in breaking free than had his human self. Raurí glared at the offending rope and had to prevent himself from giving vent to a frustrated growl.

He drew back his lips in a silent snarl and in frustration attacked the ropes that bound him so securely. Furiously the beast gnawed and fibres parted under that assault. Hemp rope was not manufactured to withstand razor-sharp fangs.

In a short time the fearsome beast was free from its bonds and dropped to all fours. Raurí raised his snout to the sky and had to restrain himself from howling in triumph. Cautiously he looked along the line of prisoners fastened to the wall. Wrapped up in their own misery no one noticed the extraordinary materialization of a massive wolf inside the courtyard.

Keeping to the shadows, the wolf padded silently towards the door leading to the living quarters. Once inside, Raurí stood sniffing the miscellany of odours within the building, his ears cocked as he tried to orientate himself. The drunken revelry drowned out all other noise. Raurí sorted through the smells until he located those spiced with gun oil and cartridges and weapons of death then padded through the corridors towards his goal.

He might have made it undetected only a drunken constable decided at that moment to stagger into the passage, hand over mouth as he tried to hold in the vomit threatening to erupt before he got to the latrines.

The man gaped in surprise, his nausea momentarily on hold, as he saw what he imagined to be a huge dog coming towards him. The fright engendered by the terrifying sight lasted only momentarily and then he opened his mouth to yell.

Whatever sound emerged from the constable's throat was drowned out by the carousing coming from the room he had just left. But by then it did not matter, for the great beast leapt forward, crashing into the constable and throwing him backwards on to the unyielding stone floor. The last thing he saw was a gaping maw filled with teeth just before his throat was ripped out.

Raurí crouched by the body, his senses alert, but there was no further excursions from the mess hall. Gripping the shoulder of the dead man in his bloodstained fangs, he dragged the corpse along the corridor until he came to the place he had been seeking. He pawed the door open and dragged the body inside. For moments he crouched there, listening for further movements from his foe, but the revelry from the carousing police company carried on as before. It was then he decided he could better carry out his plan in his human form.

When the transformation was complete, he inspected the armoury, taking stock of the weapons stacked on the wooden racks. He closed the door, stripped the corpse and donned the uniform.

In his guise as a police officer, Raurí selected the items he needed. A couple of bayonets stuffed into his belt. He grabbed up rifles and slung them from his shoulders. Revolvers he also took and stuffed in his belt. Lastly he selected a quantity of grenades and cramming some in his pockets carried a couple more in his hands. Overly laden with weaponry he emerged from the room. Then potential disaster, as the door to the dining area opened and a man staggered out. Raurí cursed under his breath but carried on walking, his head lowered.

"Where the hell are you going?"

Another man emerged and frowned as he saw one of his comrades coming towards him festooned with arms.

"What the bloody hell's going on?"

Raurí knew exactly what he had to do. As he reached the men he swung his fist at the last one to emerge. The constable was too befuddled with drink to take evasive action. The grenade in Raurí's hand lent weight and effectiveness to the blow and the man was punched sideways hitting his head against the wall and falling unconscious to the floor. His companion gaped at Raurí and opened his mouth to shout.

Again a grenade-laden fist lashed out, hitting the constable in the mouth and breaking his jaw. As the man went down Raurí kicked him in the face. The policeman rolled over and dribbling blood crawled across the corridor.

Dropping the grenade Raurí pulled out a bayonet and stabbed the peeler in the back of the neck. The injured man squealed; his hands and feet slipping on the stone floor in his haste to get away.

Again and again Raurí stabbed his victim until with a final conclusive shudder the wounded man ceased moving. Turning back to the first man he had downed, Raurí reached over and sawed at his throat with the bayonet. Blood squirted out on the man's tunic and on the floor.

Breathing heavily Raurí stared at the carnage in the hallway. At any moment the door could open and more police emerge. He had to divert or delay them in some way. Dropping to his knees beside the first man he wrapped his lifeless fingers around a grenade. He then hooked the pin over a button and dropped the body back to its resting place. Swiftly he repeated the same procedure with the second dead man. He was hoping when they were discovered by their comrades, they would lift the men up to render assistance. It wasn't foolproof but even if only one of the grenades fired it would be enough.

He ran outside, the rifles clanking against his sides and hurried across the courtyard. Reaching the first prisoner, Raurí sawed at his bonds with a bayonet.

"What...?"

The prisoner was gaping at the policeman.

"Hush, it's me, Raurí. Take this bayonet and free the rest."

It did not take long before the prisoners were at liberty and gathered, shivering and naked around Raurí.

"How the hell did you do it, Raurí?"

"We thought we were goners."

"You're a bloody genius, Raurí."

"There's no one to stop us getting away now."

Raurí was busy sharing out the weapons.

"We're not getting away just yet," he told them. "There's a little matter of justice for Major Foyle."

"What do you mean?"

Raurí hefted the revolver he had kept for himself.

"The bastards that murdered Ivor are in there celebrating their victory. There was no court, no trial, no appeal, no justice. They tortured the major and then murdered him. It was a lynching. The guilty must pay for their crime."

"You mean..."

"I mean there is a nest of rodents in there," Raurí cut in harshly. "I say we go in there and clean them out. Who's with me?"

"By God, Raurí, we're all with you. It was terrible what they did to the major. Making him sit in that window naked. I couldn't look at his shame."

"The bastards promised to let him go if I told them where I had stashed the weapons. When I told them what they wanted to know, they hanged him."

"They're not lawmen at all. They're criminals in uniforms."

"That's right. Let's get the bastards."

"It'll send a message out to all the other traitors in the RIC they aren't above the law."

"Let's do it."

Raurí's men were suddenly transformed. Earlier, they had been bleakly contemplating a horrific death at the hands of the brutal Sergeant Maguire. Now, armed and filled with vengeful wrath, they were eager to follow their leader and mete out justice to the men who had treated them and their comrades so cruelly. As they marched purposefully across the courtyard Raurí told them about the booby-trapped bodies.

"Don't disturb them or you'll get your bollix blown off."

With Raurí in the lead in his RIC uniform, the rebels cautiously moved into the main building. The sounds of revelry were just as loud if not louder. They crowded into the corridor and saw the dead policemen lying undisturbed outside the mess hall.

"Remember, don't touch them."

"You're a cunning bugger, Captain. Who would have thought of using a dead man as a weapon?"

"Which just goes to show, even a dead peeler has his uses."

Raurí pointed down the corridor.

"That's where the armoury is. Those without a weapon go and arm yourselves."

In a short time a group of naked men, armed with the latest weapons, gathered in the corridor. Raurí grinned wolfishly and raised his revolver.

"For Major Foyle."

His men stared grimly back at him.

"For Major Foyle."

Someone inside the mess room was singing. The song ended to be replaced by the din of applause and laughter and catcalls.

"How do we do this?" someone asked.

Raurí stared bleakly at the speaker.

"No quarter."

"No quarter, it is then."

Raurí took out a grenade and pulled the pin before nodding towards the door. With a revolver in one hand and the grenade in the other he stepped inside. There were upwards of thirty officers scattered around the benches and tables. The air was thick with tobacco smoke while the strong odour of alcohol added to the fug.

The few constables that looked up as the door opened saw only a fellow officer and were mystified as to why he was carrying a revolver. They watched in puzzlement as he drew back his arm and tossed something towards them. Too late they recognized what it was.

One man managed to rise to his feet and shout a warning. The grenade bounced on a table and rolled to the edge before toppling on to the floor. Befuddled by the large quantities of alcohol they had imbibed, the policemen stared in puzzlement at the grenade, not registering what it implied.

When the grenade went off, the explosion was thunderous in the enclosed space of the room. The constables closest to the detonation were thrown from their benches crying out as shrapnel tore into their bodies.

The singing was abruptly cut off as the drunken officers registered what was happening. They turned to the door as the rest of Rauri's squad crowded inside. A silence fell amongst the revellers and they stared fearfully at the armed and naked men. The only noise was the moaning of the wounded.

"I find you all collectively guilty of the murder of Major Foyle," Rauri called out. "As an officer of the Irish Republican Army, I order your execution by firing squad, to be carried out with immediate effect. You have a few minutes to make your peace with God, but I doubt he will have any more mercy that me."

"Damn your black hearts," a voice roared out. "By authority of the King George of England and Ireland I order you to drop your arms at once and surrender. If you do so it might go easier at your trial."

"What trial did you give Major Foyle? You tortured and murdered him. By the same standards of justice we sentence you. But we are more humane than you callous beasts. We'll leave out the torture. Now say your prayers and prepare to die."

"Rush them, men. They won't dare shoot."

There was a general stirring amongst the police constables as they heard the order. They hesitated, staring in apprehension at the armed men. They were defenceless and the thought of tackling armed men was a daunting prospect. They were also very drunk.

Sergeant Maguire had been edging back behind his men, even as he urged them to attack. Rauri took careful aim and fired at the big sergeant. His shot was shocking loud inside the room. Maguire jerked as the round hit him then disappeared from view as he fell back. Rauri's shot stunned everyone in the room—both police and rebels. Everyone froze.

"Fire at will," Rauri yelled and suiting words to action loosed shots into the men cowering before them.

It was as if he had thrown a switch. His men immediately triggered their purloined weapons. Every man had a rifle or a revolver and one even had a machinegun. They unleashed a veritable storm of lead.

All the pain and humiliation and blows and kicks and insults from their captors had built up in them a well of hate and resentment. There was no mercy in their hearts as they fired at the men who had brutalized them and murdered their beloved major.

They fired, and the weapons grew hot in their hands as their victims cowered in that room of death. Some tried to overturn tables and chairs and shelter behind them. But that was no avail as their killers tossed grenades in amongst the survivors. It was total carnage and the firing went on and on until hammers clicked on empty. Smoke from the weapons drifted into the room smothering the tobacco and alcohol fumes.

CHAPTER TWENTY-SIX

Benedict Phelan drove away from the barracks, accompanied by McCrudden, Captain Mac Cathail's former sergeant.

"That was a bloody good night's work. We have settled a score with Mac Cathail and we get our guns back. Is there anything we have missed? I don't want any loose ends. The last time few times we had dealings with Mac Cathail he turned up again, causing all sorts of trouble. However, this time he is safe in the police barracks. We shan't have any more trouble with that slippery bastard."

"There are two members of that crowd that haven't been accounted for; Damian Hughes and Aishling O'Hagan."

"Aishling O'Hagan. I owe that bitch. She threw me over for Mac Cathail. I didn't like that, one bit."

"The thing is, she can finger me," McCrudden said. "It won't take her long to figure out who betrayed them. If that information gets out, I'll have a Dublin Death Squad after me."

"Jeez, Malachi, if they know about you they'll probably be able to link me with tonight's business as well." For a moment they drove in silence. "It's no good. We have to make sure. I don't want to live the rest of my life wondering when there'll be a knock on the door. We'll have to go after those two and hope they haven't told anyone about tonight's shenanigans.

"Here's what we do. You go to Aishling O'Hagan and tell her Mac Cathail is badly hurt and gone into hiding in that old deserted croft in the Moneymore bog. Round up a few of the boys and send them out there to lie in wait for the bitch. Take some rope and tie her up until I have a chance to deal with her. We can have a bit of fun with the bitch before we dispose of her. I'll go for Hughes and tell him the same tale. They can join the other bodies in the bog. Where will I be likely to get hold of Hughes?"

"I've seen him at Foyle's creamery. The major gave him a job and the freak spends most of his time there."

"Off you go then. Once we've disposed of the bitch and the freak I need to get back to the barracks. I want to be there when Maguire deals with Mac Cathail. Today we tie up any loose ends and then we'll be free of Mac Cathail and his damned rebels once and for all."

• • •

Ina answered the door to McCrudden.

"I need to speak to Aishling, it's urgent."

"She's fast asleep. What's it about?"

"It's about Raurí Mac Cathail. Please, I need to see her. Can't you wake her?"

"What about Raurí?"

"He's badly hurt, but we've took him to a safe place. He keeps calling for Aishling. I didn't want to leave him but I think he needs more help than I can give."

"Come in. I'll wake Aishling."

The girl came in sleepily rubbing her eyes. Her tiredness fell away as she saw who the visitor was.

"What's happening?"

"The whole thing was a trap. Someone betrayed us. I was delayed so I wasn't in on the start of the raid. It was lucky I was. When I came up and realized what was happening I started shooting. It created enough of a diversion to enable Raurí to fight his way out of the barracks. I think some of the boys were wounded or maybe even killed. It was all happening so fast I didn't have time to figure out what all was going on. Some of us got away but Raurí took a bullet. We managed to get him away. He's pretty bad. I've sent someone for a doctor but I'm not sure if anyone will attend him. They're supposed to report things like that to the peelers. I'm sorry; I didn't know what else to do. Raurí keeps calling out your name."

"Oh, dear God, I'll have to go to him. Is he alone?"

"No, I left some of the boys with him. They're looking after him until we get there."

"I'll get some things and then we'll go."

In a short time Aishling had pulled on an outdoor cloak and was carrying a small bag.

"I've packed some dressings. I can treat him as best I can and then we can decide if he's fit enough to be moved back here."

● ● ●

The creamery looked deserted as Phelan parked his truck and clambered from the cab. There were luminous streaks in the horizon as dawn struggled to light up the world.

"Hello, anyone at home?" he called, banging on the front door.

"Yes, what do you want?" The voice came from other side of the yard.

Phelan put his hand on the revolver inside his jacket. He could just make out the figure at the corner of the house.

"Damian, thank goodness I found you. Your friend Raurí has been hurt. He needs help."

"Raurí hurt; what happened? Where is he?"

"There was a shootout with the peelers. Raurí was wounded during a raid or something. I don't know any details and I don't want to know. A friend of mine has taken him somewhere safe. But he needs assistance. I don't want to get involved but I owe this friend a favour. He asked me to fetch you. Said as you would help. I'll take you to him but more than that I can't do. I can't risk getting mixed up in anything like this."

By now Phelan had his gun out, holding it by his side, out of sight of Damian.

"Come into the light. I can't see you there."

Damian was suspicious. He knew Phelan was lying but was curious as to what his game was. If Raurí was hurt or in danger the man might be tricked into saying something that would give Damian a clue as to what he was up to. Damian stepped out into the yard.

"Where is he?"

"Moneymore bog; there's an old shack. No one ever goes there, so he should be safe. But he does need all the help he can get." While he was talking the big man was moving towards Damian. "You want to jump in the truck and I'll take you there. Raurí and I have never been the best of friends but when a fellow's in trouble, Benedict is the man to help."

Damian was watchful, speculating what the gangster was up to; wondering if he should indeed go with him, but thinking maybe he wouldn't, for Phelan was a treacherous snake. After all, Damian had witnessed him beat Raurí to a pulp, leaving him for dead. He had no reason to think Phelan's offer of help was other than a trick.

"I'd better get my coat."

Damian turned towards the front door. Phelan raised the firearm and pointed it at Damian's back.

"Good idea, Damian. It's a cold night to be out and about. But it's colder in the grave."

He squeezed the trigger. The bullets hit Damian and punched him forward, slamming him into the door—his hands scrabbling at the wood panels as he tried to stay upright. But the bullets kept coming and he crumpled to the ground, an untidy heap of humanity. Phelan walked forward and kicked the lifeless figure.

"Someone should have put you out of your misery years ago, you freak," Phelan observed as he reloaded.

He turned and walked back to his truck, climbed aboard, reversed out of the yard and drove off, leaving a cloud of exhaust smoke to mix with the reek of cordite. There was also the sweet coppery smell of blood seeping on to the cobbles from the motionless body slumped by the door.

Somewhere a dog barked and cows mournfully called from the fields waiting to be taken in for milking.

• • •

"Not much further now."

Aishling did not answer. Her mind was filled with dread for Raurí. She had questioned her guide about Raurí's condition but McCrudden had been elusive, confessing he was not that familiar with bullet wounds but there had been a lot of blood. They had to carry Raurí for he was too weak to walk. She also quizzed him about the raid.

"It was a trap. The few of us that got away were the lucky ones. I saw some of our comrades gunned down. I don't know how they found out about the raid. It was terrible. It was as if they were waiting for us."

"That Sergeant Maguire, he has spies everywhere," Aishling observed, bitterly. "He called at our house once to put pressure on Ina; wanted to recruit her as an informer; told her to report anyone that came to her to be treated for injuries. "

"Yeah, he is a mean bastard. I wouldn't like to get on the wrong side of him."

Aishling frowned at this, thinking McCrudden was very much on the wrong side of Sergeant Maguire, seeing as he had attacked the police barracks.

SOMEWHERE A DOG BARKED AND COWS MOURNFULLY CALLED FROM THE FIELDS...

"Was anyone captured?"

"I don't know. There was so much confusion with guns going off all around, and us trying to get away, I couldn't see what was happening to anyone else. I was too busy holding on to Raurí. He was able to keep going for a while and then he just collapsed. In the end we had to carry him."

Dawn was struggling to be seen behind the dark clouds that mirrored Aishling's gloomy thoughts. There were pathways through Moneymore bog, but outside of these, the marsh held treacherous patches for the unwary. For a moment Aishling wondered at this choice of hideaway for the wounded Raurí. It seemed a long way from the barracks.

There was something about McCrudden's story that was not quite right, but Aishling was unable to figure out what it was that bothered her. She was too agitated to think straight, worrying about Raurí; wondering how badly he was injured and mulling over the ways and means to get him back to Ina's where they could look after him.

"Are you armed?" McCrudden suddenly asked.

"No." It had never entered her head to arm herself. She was on a mission of mercy and had seen no reason to take along her gun. "Why do you ask?"

"Oh, no reason, it's just the peelers might be hunting for survivors. Don't want to give them an excuse to haul us in."

At last the shack came in sight. McCrudden's smile was strained as he turned to her.

"You go on in. I'll stay out here and make sure we weren't followed."

She pushed the rickety door open. It creaked alarmingly. She could sense someone there.

"Raurí."

There was movement to one side and a musty fabric was thrown over her. Aishling tried to duck away but a pair of brawny arms wrapped around her, restricting her movements. She kicked out and fought but it was hopeless from the very start. There were more than one attacker and they smothered her in the thick smelly cloth so her punches and kicks were deadened in the fabric. The thick blanket tightened about her and she felt the ropes being wrapped around and even as she struggled she was pushing out her arms and legs to keep the bindings loose. She was given a violent push and fell to the floor, cocooned inside the cloth and helpless; not knowing who her attackers were; knowing only it was McCrudden who had led her into the trap.

In spite of her own predicament the thought uppermost in Aishling's mind was the anxiety she felt for Raurí. If McCrudden was a traitor, he must then have betrayed Raurí. And she wept for her lover not knowing his fate.

CHAPTER TWENTY-SEVEN

As the gun smoke drifted through the room a terrible silence descended. It lasted only moments before being broken by the sound of retching. Two of the volunteers were bent over, venting the contents of their stomachs. For most it was their first taste of bloodletting and the white faces and vacant stares of the rest of the band was evidence of this. Raurí turned to his men and held up his hand for attention.

"I want to congratulate you on your performance over the last several hours. In spite of your capture and vicious beating at the hands of the peelers you rallied enough to strike back. You have wiped out the enemy and deserve to go home to a well-earned rest. I would not ask any more from you, for you have done more than many other men might have ever achieved in a lifetime of soldiering. Major Foyle would have been proud of you for he loved you dearly. Each and every one of you had a special place in his affection.

"I will think no less of you if you decide you have done enough and decline the next task. There is a complete armoury in this building and there are two lorries outside. We have the opportunity to loot the barracks. We can drive the weapons to a place of safekeeping." Raurí pointed to his dark green Royal Irish Constabulary uniform. "In order to do this and deceive anyone who might think to challenge us, I ask you if you are willing to do this one final thing; to disguise your true identity and put on police uniforms. That way we may be able to bluff our way past army or police patrols."

Raurí paused, allowed his words to sink in. Their reaction took him by surprise. Someone began to laugh, more a giggle than a proper laugh. The mirth spread. Suddenly everyone was laughing and calling out suggestions.

"We be driving around in peeler's uniforms!"

"Hey, we could arrest a few drunks."

"What about shooting some of those IRA rebels."

"We could go in the public houses and have free drinks.

"What a jape! When I get home I'll frighten the life out of my auld ma."

As they clowned around, the tension eased and they became animated and mischievous, slapping each other on the back or joining in mock wrestling.

"All right, all right!" Raurí yelled above the hubbub. "Enough of this tomfoolery. We better get started. I want a man outside on watch. We don't want to be surprised by a patrol rolling up and catching you with your pants down."

In high spirits the men rushed to do Raurí's bidding. It was with great glee they broke into the personal lockers of dead constables and plundered the contents. The locker room was pandemonium as the recruits tried on various articles of police uniforms.

"These trousers are too big for me. He must have been a right fat bastard."

"Those goombeens ware all well fed. That's why most of them are in the job. They had nothing before they joined and then suddenly they can thieve and plunder with the might of the law behind them."

"When we have our republic I'm going to join the peelers."

"Yeah, but they won't be called peelers; that's after Robert Peel who was an Englishman. It'll have to be something Irish."

"What about Collins after Michael Collins?"

"Watch out here come the Collins."

They clowned and chuckled and kitted themselves out as passable members of the Royal Irish Constabulary. Clad in their new outfits they looted the barracks, loading weaponry and ammunition on one of the lorries. Raurí had trouble restraining them from setting the place on fire.

"The smoke will be seen for miles. Someone is bound to come and investigate. Let's finish up here and get as far away as possible. Only one thing remains and that is to recover the major's body. When this is over we'll give him a proper funeral."

Laden with booty and in high spirits the little band of rebels drove away from the barracks at Mullentoone, leaving behind an eerily quiet building, with the former inhabitants lying in their own gore in the wreckage of the dining hall, where they had gathered to celebrate the hanging of a rebel chieftain and the anticipated torture and execution of his band of followers.

● ● ●

Aishling lay very still listening intently as the men outside greeted someone.

"Did you get the bitch?"

"Sure thing, Benedict, she's inside trussed up like a Sunday roast."

The door opened and footsteps came inside. A heavy boot thudded into her side.

"Hello, bitch, I hear you been out raiding police barracks with your boyfriend. I always knew you'd come to a bad end."

The blanketed figure sobbed loudly.

"Please, please, I never did nothing to you. Please let me go home. My grandma will be worried about me."

Loud guffaws and another brutal kick.

"Jeez, I forgot about that auld witch. Did Ina see you?"

"Do you think it matters?"

"Maybe not. You can always make up some story if she ever asks. You can always say you took the bitch to Mac Cathail but then never saw them again."

"Yeah, you're probably right. What about Damian Hughes? Did you find him?"

"Sure I did."

"Where is he? What have you done with him?"

"I did what someone should have done years ago. I put six good ones in him."

"Jeez, Benedict, what did he do?"

"He dropped down dead as a dodo."

There were howls of laughter. Aishling lay still, shocked by what she had heard. There were the sounds of men horsing around thumping each other and letting out yowls of mirth.

"Ah, that's a good one, Benedict."

"Anyway, we haven't time to mess with the bitch now. We got to check those arms are where Mac Cathail said they were. Then we have to get back to the barracks. Maguire's putting on a show for us. This piece of fresh meat will keep for a while longer. Won't you, darling?"

Aishling wailed like a woman demented, her cries going up a notch or two as she was subjected to more kicking.

"Howl away there, Aishling. When we come back we'll give you something to howl about. At least you'll go out of this world happy with half a dozen good men and true lining up to pleasure you."

With one final kick at his helpless victim Phelan left, slamming the door shut behind him.

CHAPTER TWENTY-EIGHT

The smugglers found the arms where Raurí had said they were. Phelan did a quick inventory.

"That bastard, Mac Cathail, it's not all here."

"He would have taken some to carry out the attack on the barracks."

"A man can't make an honest living with them thieving rebels around," Phelan said passionately. "All the trouble he caused me, he deserves whatever fate Maguire has in store for him. I'm looking forward to seeing him hang. Did you see Mac Cathail's face when the old rebel was kicked out the window? I just hope they don't start without us. I want to watch that waster suffer and listen to him scream."

"Oh, he'll scream all right. Maguire is expert at making people scream."

"Seeing as Mac Cathail and his rebels are prisoners, there's no urgency to move this stuff. Let's get back to the barracks and watch Maguire play with Mac Cathail. Afterwards we'll go back to Moneymore and have some fun with his bitch."

The smugglers clambered aboard their lorry and headed back to the barracks. There was no guard on the gate which puzzled Phelan but perhaps there was no need for a sentry as Sergeant Maguire had the rebels securely hog-tied inside.

"Let's go. I'm looking forward to this."

There was no police presence inside the yard but more disconcerting was the absence of prisoners.

"What the hell's going on here?"

Phelan had a nasty feeling Maguire had not waited for him before disposing of Mac Cathail and his band.

"Hello, anyone about."

The shouts echoed eerily around the empty yard.

"Some of you check the outbuildings while I go inside and see if I can find out what the hell's going on. There's something wrong here."

Inside the main building Phelan saw the bodies of the dead policemen sprawled in the corridor and smelt the cordite. He drew his pistol and edged slowly to the doorway. The smell of blood was thick in the room mixed with the stink of burnt gunpowder. The place was a shambles, with broken and splintered benches and tables and the mangled remains of men blown to pieces with their own grenades. Phelan reeled from the sight.

"In here," he yelled.

They piled inside, coming to a halt when they caught sight of the dead bodies in the corridor.

"Holy god, what the…!"

"In there." Phelan gestured to the room beyond. "They're all dead."

His men crowded into the doorway, staring in disbelief at the carnage. Someone began to retch.

"Oh, dear God. The poor bastards."

"No sign of Mac Cathail?"

"Nothing. The place is empty. There's cut ropes lying in the yard. Someone must have freed them and they slaughtered the whole garrison.

"Let's get out of here."

They fled the building; as if afraid the dead policemen would suddenly come to life and accuse them of being involved in their deaths. Running across the courtyard, the smugglers fought to get through the gate and out to the lorry waiting to ferry them away from this dreadful place manned by dead peelers. As they clambered on board they heard the sound of vehicles. In the act of starting the engine Phelan paused and stared apprehensively as he spied the army lorries. Phelan groaned. The irony of their situation did not escape him—armed men driving away from a barracks full of murdered policemen.

"Hide your guns," he called urgently.

He tucked his own revolver beneath the seat and jumped down on the road, his hands held out from his sides. The army wagons pulled up and soldiers climbed out, dispersing to each side of the road. A dozen or so rifles pointing at Phelan's gang. More tenders were arriving even as the first lot deployed.

"Throw down your weapons! And stand away from the vehicle."

"Do as he says," Phelan called to his men. "For bloody sake get down real slow." He walked towards the soldiers. "Thank God you've come. Something terrible has happened."

"Identify yourselves."

"Benedict Phelan. I'm a friend of Sergeant Maguire, or was a friend. We've just found them—all shot to pieces. It's a slaughterhouse in there."

More and more soldiers were arriving and deploying around the smugglers' lorry.

"Lie on the ground—arms and legs spread."

There was no other choice. They did as they were ordered. While this was going on other soldiers were entering the barracks.

"I tell you, I'm a friend of Maguire," Phelan persisted. "He invited us back here for a celebration. We helped him capture a bunch of rebels. He wanted me to witness their interrogation."

Phelan looked up into the muzzle of an army pistol being held by the English officer glowering down at him.

"While you're holding us here the rebels are escaping."

A soldier emerged from the gate.

"Sir, you ought to see this. It's a bloodbath in there."

At that moment there came a muffled explosion from inside the barracks. Someone was screaming.

"What the hell was that?"

The screaming continued.

"Keep this scum covered. Shoot if they make a wrong move."

The officer disappeared through the gate.

"This is all a mistake," Phelan protested. "We found the place like this. We were going for help."

A rifle barrel was jammed into the small of his back.

"Shut up. If it was up to me I'd shoot the bloody lot of you rebels."

Phelan lay quiet until he heard the officer return.

"I can't believe it. The whole garrison murdered. You lot are for hanging or I'll resign my commission."

The growing sounds of an engine made everyone look up. Phelan craned to see who was arriving now. A Model T car rolled up and parked. A soldier jumped out, opened the rear door then stood to attention. Phelan watched as an officer stepped out from the car.

"Good show, Captain Lawson, I see you captured the rebels. Give you any bother?"

"Major Bullock, sir!" The captain saluted smartly. "This lot were about to make a getaway when we arrived."

"Well done, captain." Major Bullock turned and gazed in the direction of the barracks. "What's the situation inside? Why haven't the police garrison shown themselves?"

"The whole garrison has been wiped out, sir. I doubt anyone is left alive. I have men inside going through the place. They have to be very careful. It looks like the bastards left booby-traps. One of my men was injured when he disturbed a body."

"Bloody savages! I'd rather fight fuzzy-wuzzies as chase these Irish gutter rats. Hang the lot of them and be done with it. No matter how many we shoot, more keep crawling out of the bogs."

A pair of highly polished boots appeared beside Phelan. A toe prodded him none too gently.

"What have you to say for yourself, fellow? Can you speak English or do you speak that incomprehensible gobbledygook you blether in this godforsaken country?"

"Major, you're making a terrible mistake. I keep trying to tell the captain here, we were on our way to raise the alarm. It was a gang under the leadership of a notorious rebel who calls himself Captain Mac Cathail. I helped Sergeant Maguire capture them. We left on an errand for the sergeant. We were on our way back to assist with the interrogation of the prisoners. While we were gone the rebels broke free and murdered those poor brave peelers."

"I'm sure you are lying. You murdered those poor fellows and now you are making up some cock and bull story."

"This is stupid. If we killed those poor bastards in there why are our weapons unfired?"

"What are you talking about?"

"Our guns—they're in our lorry. They've never been fired. Take a look. Sergeant Maguire was a friend. I helped him capture those rebels. They were tied up in the yard. Someone cut them free. You can see the cut ropes lying in there in the courtyard."

Phelan was talking fast, knowing he was in a tight situation. He had to convince the soldiers he was on their side.

"Captain," the major said at last. "Search the fellow's vehicle and examine any weapons you find. If this fellow is telling the truth I don't want to lose the chance of catching the perpetrators of this massacre. I'm going inside to see for myself."

There came another explosion from the barracks. Everyone looked up expectantly but this time there was no screaming.

"Another bloody booby-trap, no doubt," the captain muttered. "Bloody savages! I hope no one caught it that time."

Footsteps were heard approaching. All attention was on the gate as stretcher bearers manoeuvred their burden through. Major Bullock stepped forward.

"How is he?"

"Really bad, sir. Got it in the face and chest. Grenade under the body, primed to go off when moved. We're using ropes to keep our distance when moving the others. Pretty grisly in there."

"Thank you, anyone left alive?"

"Nary a one, sir. All blown to kingdom come."

"I'm going in to have a look myself."

"If you don't mind a bit of advice, sir, don't touch anything. God knows what else they've set up in there."

"I'll be careful. Captain, you have a look for those weapons. I shan't be long."

The major disappeared through the gate and soldiers searched Phelan's lorry. They piled the guns on the road and awaited the major's return. Several minutes later he returned.

"Messy business—poor bastards blown to smithereens. Reminds one of Arras in France. Bloody bad business. Well, Captain, I see you found the weapons."

"Yes, sir, it's as he says—they've not been fired."

"Mmm... let the prisoners stand."

Phelan and his men were lined up against the side of the lorry. Major Bullock had a narrow face with a sparse wisp of a moustache. Cold piercing eyes bored into Phelan's.

"I found the ropes cut as you said. Perhaps you are telling the truth, or at least your version of it. Now tell me what you know about this damned affair."

Phelan felt the major could tell if he lied and he mostly kept to the truth. When he had finished, Bullock strode up and down with a thoughtful expression in his narrow face.

"This Mac Cathail chap—where are we likely to find him?"

"I'm not sure where that wily fox will go to ground, but as soon as I discovered he had escaped I sent a couple of men out to detain his woman. I've instructed them to take her to an old shack in the Moneymore bog. I was hoping to question her to find out where her boyfriend might be."

"His woman, you say?"

"Indeed, sir, she was part of the attacking force."

"You think you can get her to tell you where this Mac Cathail fellow is hiding out?"

"We might have to rough her up a bit but she'll talk all right."

"Mmm...."

Bullock paced up and down looking thoughtful. At last he came to some conclusion.

"Captain, how many men have we got?"

"Sir, there were fifty when we set out. A few are taking Private Morrison to hospital."

"So if we leave enough here to guard the barracks we could muster at least forty. Very good! This fellow Phelan will take us to this Moneymore place. Confiscate their weapons and put a couple of our chaps in the lorry with them."

With the roaring of engines and the smell of petrol fumes the army vehicles drove away from the barracks.

CHAPTER TWENTY-NINE

Raurí stood within the trees and scanned the area around the creamery sensing something wasn't right. Cautiously he stepped from cover and walked slowly into the yard. The front door was open which wasn't unusual. Everything appeared normal until he spotted the dark stain by the front door. It was then he drew his revolver.

Slowly he stepped forward, peering through the open door, wondering what was lurking inside. The dark stain continued over the stoop and on to the stone tiles. Raurí stepped inside avoiding the stain, recognizing what it was and having a good idea whose blood it was.

The dark wash became fainter as it trailed towards the fireplace and there it ended at a huddle of clothing as if someone had thrown the garments in a heap while they attended to some more urgent task.

"Damian." Raurí knelt by the still form, his heart beating exceptionally fast. "Damian," he whispered. "Oh, Damian, who has done this to you?" He rested his cheek against the pale face, so cold like the marble statues in the local chapel. "I have lost so much, now to find I have lost my dearest friend. This is too much to bear."

There was a faint movement from Damian followed by a long sigh. Raurí stared, his own breathing on hold.

"Damian, can you hear me?"

The eyes fluttered open. Raurí had never noticed how long Damian's eyelashes were and his eyes so big, almost like a girl. The youngster was lying on his side, his legs drawn up to his chest, his back a dark mass of blood.

"Raurí." The name came out as a sigh. "I was worried about you."

A lump came in Raurí's throat. He sensed Damian was not far from death and he felt tears swell in his eyes.

"Who did this to you?"

"It... doesn't matter. How is the major? Did you find him?"

"They hung him. There was nothing I could do."

"I'm sorry, Rauri. He was the best of men."

"He was the best of men. Tell me who shot you. I killed the peelers that murdered Uncle Ivor. I'll find the ones that did this to you and execute them too."

"Don't worry about me." The words whispered. "You... you stay... safe."

"You got to tell me who it was that shot you. Someone is killing everyone close to me. They'll go after Aishling next. You got to tell me."

"Oh, Rauri... you think so?"

"It's not what I think, it's what is happening. My parents, Uncle Ivor, now you. Aishling is all I have left. I have to protect her. So if you care about me or Aishling then tell me."

"Perhaps you're right." The words faint, almost inaudible. "Benedict Phelan. He came here—told me you were hurt and needed help."

"Phelan, always Phelan," Rauri said bitterly. "It was him and his friends who beat me up that time you rescued me. He boasted about it when the peelers had me tied up at the barracks. From day one he's been the cause of all my troubles. He can't be allowed to carry on wrecking people's lives."

"Be careful, Rauri... he's dangerous."

"I don't suppose you have any idea where he was going when he left here."

"He did say something..."

Rauri had to lean close in order to make out the laboured speech.

"He said something about you taking refuge in Moneymore bog."

"Moneymore—you sure?" There was no immediate answer. "Damian?"

"I love you, Rauri."

"I love you, Damian. You are my best friend. You are more. You are my brother."

There was no response. Damian had spoken for the last time. And kneeling there, Rauri wept. Wiping his face he sat back on his heels.

"Benedict Phelan, you have destroyed my family. Three times you have tried to kill me and failed. There will be no more chances. I vow by the body of my dead friend, Damian, you will not live beyond this day."

Rauri dipped his finger in the congealing blood and traced a cross on the hearth by Damian's head.

"When next we meet only one of us will walk away."

Rauri fetched a blanket from the bedrooms and covered the body. He now had two people to bury—his Uncle Ivor and his friend Damian.

● ● ●

Like some flimsy garment carelessly tossed outside, a low mist hung over Moneymore bog. Raurí crouched in the cover of a small bunch of stunted oaks and scrutinized the marsh. He noted the disturbance of mud where a group of men had come through. From the prints he figured at least half a dozen or more in the band.

Damian said Phelan had told him that this was where Raurí was hiding out. Why mention the place at all? But then Phelan had intended killing Damian so whatever the purpose of mentioning it would be nullified when he shot Damian.

Cautiously Raurí followed the tracks, scanning every bush and tree and getting a sense of decay and neglect about the place. He spotted the old shack. It looked abandoned but he could see the recently trampled mud around the doorway.

Raurí squatted down and examined the derelict. There was no sign of life and he moved closer. A large rusty bolt pushed through a crude hasp was still in place, indicating that whoever had been there had left, seeing as the door was fastened from the outside. He eased the bolt out of its housing and pushed it open.

There was very little light inside and that came mostly from the doorway now that he had opened it. The only items he could make out in the general gloom were a crude table, a few wooden crates and a bundle of bedding in one corner. Raurí stepped inside, sensing too late the movement from behind. Someone landed on his back and he was flung forward.

A pair of hands closed on his neck. As he struggled against the choke grip he recognized the scent coming from his attacker. Almost at the same time the pressure on his neck eased.

"Raurí, is it really you?"

"Aishling."

"Oh Raurí, they told me you were captured at the barracks and were going back there to watch you hang."

Lying on the dirt floor, they embraced and hugged until they were both breathless. The world around them faded. The war with England receded. The dingy hut could have been the finest hotel, the dirt floor on which they rested a soft bed with scented sheets. It would have made no difference. For long moments they lay wrapped together.

"Who were they?" he asked but he had guessed already.

"Phelan and his gang. McCrudden lured me here, telling me you were wounded and hiding out. They were waiting for me and tied me up. I managed to get free and was looking for something to break open the door when I heard you outside. I thought they had come back to rape me. That's what they were talking about doing when they left."

"McCrudden—that snake in the grass. I have a score to settle with him *and* Phelan. Phelan murdered Damian. He died in my arms. Maguire had Uncle Ivor hanged. McCrudden betrayed us. They were waiting for us when we attacked the barracks. We managed to escape. Maguire and his filthy crew paid the penalty for murdering Uncle Ivor."

"Oh Raurí, this is a wicked war. Irishman fighting the English is bad enough, but Irishman against Irishman! There is so much bile. Our poor country has been betrayed. We sent our young men to France to fight when England asked. Now those same English soldiers they fought alongside are killing our people. We are losing the flower of our nation in this vile conflict."

"I know. It is a bitter irony indeed. Uncle Ivor had medals from when he fought in Africa for the British Empire; now that same Empire has him murdered for daring to want freedom for Ireland."

"Oh, Raurí, let's leave this cursed place. We could go to America. There is a big fresh nation where we could make a new life and be free of all this hatred and killing."

"I can't run, Aishling. I will settle scores with Benedict Phelan and his odious lickspittle, McCrudden. Maybe when that is done I might think of leaving. Did you get any idea where Phelan was going when he left here?"

"He was on his way to the barracks to watch Maguire torture you. When he gets there he'll find out you've escaped and he'll come looking for you."

Raurí's eyes narrowed as he thought about this.

"There's a good chance once they discover what happened at the barracks they'll come back for you. We don't want to be caught out here with only this revolver between us. We need to go to ground and devise a plan to stop Phelan once and for all."

"Where can we go?"

"The creamery will be watched. Ina's place is out, for they'll expect you to go there. I had to tell Phelan the whereabouts of the weapons so we can't go there."

"What if the weapons are still there? I mean in that cave. We could arm ourselves and go hunting for Phelan instead of us hiding from him."

Raurí looked thoughtfully at his companion, slowly nodding his head.

"That makes sense. Even if they have moved the weapons we might be able to shelter in the cave until the hunt cools off. They'll probably not think of looking for us there."

"What's that?"

Aishling cocked her head to one side. Raurí listened also but could hear nothing. Aishling's senses were much keener than were Raurí's.

"Lorries—lots of lorries."

The ominous rumbling of vehicles on the move grew louder like the growling of some strange beast prowling the country lanes.

"You're right. What the hell's going on?"

And then they saw them. A ominous line of lorries advancing across the dirt roads. On they came, roaring and belching fumes. Raurí looked around but there was no place to hide. They were caught out in the open. And then it was too late as they were spotted. The engines changed tone and the drivers accelerated towards them. Shots rang out as some of the soldiers fired at them.

They took off like startled hares. Behind them they heard shouted orders. More shots followed. But the fugitives did not look around. They kept running while the roar of engines gathered pace behind them.

CHAPTER THIRTY

"We got them," Benedict Phelan crowed as he steered the lorry across the uneven ground.

Behind him streamed the army vehicles bouncing across the rough terrain, the drivers caught up in the excitement of the chase. Some of the soldiers in danger of being thrown from the careering trucks as they fired off shots at the fleeing figures.

The Model T, with Major Bullock aboard, sped ahead of the trucks. The officer had his revolver out and peered through the windscreen, a gleam of excitement on his narrow countenance. Unable to contain himself, he leaned out his window, aiming his revolver at the fugitives.

"For god's sake man, avoid the bloody bog holes!" he exclaimed, his aim spoiled by the bouncing vehicle.

It was a wild and reckless chase with everyone caught up in the excitement. Soldiers in the rear of the trucks were whooping and firing off shots even though most of them knew it was futile. The bouncing lorries were no platform for accurate shooting.

"They can't get away," Phelan yelled.

McCrudden was squeezed in the front seat beside his boss.

"We have the boogers. They're trapped in the bog and up ahead there's the Lough. This time we'll make sure Mac Cathail is dead and stays dead."

The vehicles bounced and swerved across the uneven ground, the drivers trying to avoid the worst of the tussocks of coarse grass and stunted bushes and fissures in the turf. A lorry veering to avoid a clump of briars ran into the path of the truck behind. The driver wrenched the steering wheel to avoid a collision and at the same time shammed on his brakes. There was no room for manoeuvre and the front end crunched into the side of the leading lorry. A number of soldiers from both vehicles were thrown from the trucks. Chaos followed as the trucks behind swerved and braked to avoid the crash. Captain Lawson jumped out of his vehicle, one of the fortunate few not to be involved in the pileup.

"Everyone out," he bawled. "We go on foot from here on."

Phelan's truck had come to a halt as it hit marshy ground, with the front wheels imbedded in the mud. The Model T, being lighter, was reversing out of the soft ground. Major Bullock leapt from the car and emptied his revolver in the direction of the fugitives.

"Damn bloody bad luck," the major cursed.

He turned and saw the soldiers marching towards him in good order.

"Company halt!" The captain advanced and saluted his superior. "Sir!"

"Is there any way around this quagmire?" Bullock asked Phelan.

"They have nowhere to go. We're surrounded by bog and about a mile ahead is Lough Cullenmore. They're boxed in."

"By God, that's good news. We have them then. What about this Lough— could they escape across that?"

"No way." Phelan was shaking his head. "It's fed from the sea and there are dangerous currents and rocky outcrops. It's claimed the lives of a few people. Mac Cathail would need a boat and then only an expert fisherman, familiar with the Lough, could navigate that particular stretch of water."

"This gets better and better. Captain, spread the men out in a line about twenty yards apart. I want them staggered so some are ahead of the others. That way as we move forward we're bound to scoop them up."

"If you don't mind me saying, sir, it's getting late."

Both men looked at the darkening sky.

"If we're stumbling around in the dark it's possible the fugitives might slip through."

"Damn, I want that bastard. After what he did to those policemen he mustn't get away. He has to be brought to book."

"We could camp out here, sir. Post sentries to prevent them slipping past."

"Dogs, that's what we need," Bullock mused aloud. He turned to Phelan.

"THEY HAVE NOWHERE TO GO. WE'RE SURROUNDED BY BOG..."

"You know anyone around here with dogs? Hunting dogs preferably."

"Kenny Maher keeps dogs. He uses them for hare coursing and badger baiting. People bring racing dogs to him that are past their best. Phelan sets them loose and then he'll sic his hounds on them. I've watched them take a greyhound down and rip it to pieces in less time it would take you to light a cigarette. Vicious mutts they are. He only lives a few miles from here. But he might object to bringing them out for this sort of hunt."

"Captain," the major said to Lawson, "have we anyone here familiar with hunting dogs?"

"Corporal Griffin, sir. He's from Warwickshire and helped with the hunt there."

"Tell Griffin to take five men and go with Phelan to fetch these hounds. If this fellow, Maher objects, commandeer the dogs. Tell him they are needed in the service of the crown. Take no nonsense. Arrest him if he gives any bother. Shoot him if necessary, but bring back those dogs. I don't want that bastard out there getting away. We have him bottled up here and I want nothing left to chance."

While the rest of the company set up camp, Phelan with Griffin and the five soldiers who might be needed to reinforce the corporal's authority drove off on their errand.

"What the hell's this about?" Kenny Maher was a large florid faced man who greeted his visitors suspiciously. "There are no rebels here."

"We need to borrow your dogs," Phelan told him. "The army has a couple of rebels trapped up yonder. They want you and your hounds to sniff them out."

"Can't do it."

At this point Corporal Griffin intervened. The soldier was a small man with a weather beaten face.

"You're under arrest, mister, for refusing to corporate with His Majesty's forces." He motioned to the soldiers. "Take him. Handcuff him."

"What the heck! You can't do that. I'm a loyal citizen."

"You've refused to cooperate with His Majesty's Crown Forces and that's treason. You'll probably hang. Put the cuffs on."

"Wait, wait! All right, I'll do it. But I'll want paying."

"That's fine, Mr Maher. Put in a requisition for your expenses."

Maher turned abruptly and stalked down the yard towards a row of ramshackle sheds. A cacophony of barking broke out. Corporal Griffin gripped the dogman by the arm.

"If those hounds attack any of my men, we'll shoot them."

The two men stood glaring hatred at each other.

"I can control my dogs, soldier. Just make sure you control your men."

The corporal stood back and passed a signal to his men. Weapons were readied. The dog owner unlatched the shed.

"Stay outside. I'll need to put them on leashes."

The hideous racket from within made his warning superfluous. There was no way any of the little party would have dared go inside that shed full of snarling hounds. Some minutes later Phelan emerged with his pack: six huge hounds of various hues and breeds. Fangs exposed they snarled viciously at the little knot of men nervously watching. Phelan had a thick blackthorn stick dangling from a leather throng on one wrist while in his other hand he gripped the bundle of leads.

"Quiet!" he roared.

Amazingly the noise fell away to a whimpering, but the dogs continued to glare balefully at the soldiers as if regarding them as the quarry that was to be hunted down and torn to pieces. They looked quite capable of doing just that.

The dog man walked to the army truck. With a few curt commands he loaded the dogs and climbed aboard with them. The soldiers hesitated and it was obvious they were wondering who was to travel in the back with the pack. Corporal Griffin settled the matter.

"All of you in the back. Phelan and I will travel inside. Go on. Move it!"

Reluctantly the soldiers clambered into the back of the lorry while Maher glared maliciously at them and muttered threats under his breath. Darkness was well and truly established as they travelled along the dirt roads. It was a very relieved squad of soldiers that jumped down from the lorry when they arrived back at the camp. Vehicles were scattered around the bog. The army had settled in with fires lit here and there with soldiers cooking supper, wood smoke mingling with the damp musty atmosphere of the marsh.

"Good man," Major Bullock greeted the newcomer. "You know what is expected."

"No, I don't. All I was told was to bring my dogs to hunt someone. How much am I to be paid for this night's work?"

The colonel blinked at this show of insolence, taking an instant dislike to the man.

"You will be paid the usual bounty," he said testily but didn't add, on condition the oaf succeeded in his task. "We have the fugitives bottled up, and as night is settling in I don't want them to slip past. Can you prevent that? We have sentries posted but I don't want to take a chance of them escaping."

"If you can supply me with tent pegs or stakes I'll tether my dogs at intervals along the line of your sentries. If your man comes within throwing distance of the line, my dogs will wake everyone for miles around."

The dogs were eventually spaced at intervals of a few hundred yards apart, tethered to pegs hammered into muddy ground.

"Now we only have to wait for dawn and we can release my little beauties."

Major Bullock fretted he had forgotten anything that might mean his quarry could escape. The more he thought about it the more he was convinced he had the fugitives trapped and tomorrow he would hunt them down and bring them back to be hanged for their crimes.

Benedict Phelan sat contentedly by the campfire alongside his men, relishing the morrow when at last his enemy would be cornered. If Benedict had anything to do with it, Raurí Mac Cathail would die. It was a stroke of brilliance to have brought in Maher and his dogs. Tomorrow promised to be a good day.

Maher sat and brooded over the coming hunt. In spite of his surliness and feigned reluctance to be part of the operation he was quite excited by his mission. In his life he had hunted, trapped and slaughtered every creature that walked, crawled or flew, but the one thing he had never dared hunt was a human being. He had often fantasized about it, wondering what it would be like to hunt the beast at the summit of the animal world. Tomorrow, he would have the chance to do so.

Darkness settled over the heath. Cooking fires flickered, illuminating the vehicles and the men crouched by them, drinking tea and eating bread and bacon. As soldiers finished their meal, they were sent out to relieve their comrades who were standing sentry duty while they in turn came into the fires for food washed down with steaming mugs of tea.

CHAPTER THIRTY-ONE

A few hundred yards out from the army camp the fugitives sat cross-legged facing each other. It was well past midnight and darkness lay around them like a shroud. Even though there was no chance of being seen, they sheltered in a shallow depression edged by thick clumps of rushes.

For the last few hours they had probed the defences of the army camp, seeking a way past the cordon of sentries. Each time the soldiers were forewarned of their approach by the savage barking of dogs. Shots were loosed into the night even though the soldiers could see nothing.

"Those bloody dogs—we can't get anywhere near without them sounding the alarm."

"We could try swimming the Lough?"

"I keep telling you, those are treacherous waters out there, added to which is the fact that I can't swim."

Now that night had fallen it was bitterly cold. Both were lightly dressed. For long moments they sat brooding.

"You know what will happen when they catch you?"

"They'll either kill me there and then, or take me back to be hanged."

"What do you think they will do to me?"

"I don't know. If they don't kill you then there's every possibility you'll go to prison for a very long time."

"They'll kill me as well. Phelan can't afford to let me go free. He knows I'll likely go to the leadership of the Irish Republican Army and once they know the extent of his treachery they'll go after him."

Again there was silence as they pondered the difficulties ahead.

"I love you, Raurí. I wish this was one of those nights when we would meet up and run through the fields and leys and valleys."

He moved close and took her face in his hands.

"I love you, Aishling. We'll come through this, and then we'll be together. Nothing will part us. It is only now, when I think of what might happen to you, I realize how much you mean to me."

"Hush, you foolish man; we are not finished yet. You know we have another hand to play."

"It's the one way that might give us an edge. The problem is your coat— you have the most wonderful luminous pelt when you change. You'll be noticeable even in the dark."

She stared back at him thoughtfully.

"You make a break for it then. On your own you will stand a better chance of getting through. I'll hide out as long as I can, while you bring reinforcements."

"No, I'm not leaving you behind. We both go, or we both stay. And where the hell will I find enough men to take on the soldiers camped out here? There must be forty or fifty of them, as well as Phelan's men. But there is a way to overcome the problem of your pale coat. We're in the middle of a bog, chock-full of mud. We slather your coat in mud and hey presto you become a mud turtle."

"Holy mother, I believe that might work. What about our clothes? We'll have to leave them here and they're bound to find them."

"We leave them down by the shore. They'll assume we swam out into the Lough and drowned. Either way it doesn't matter."

"Come on, let's do it."

If anyone had observed the figures by the Lough they would have been puzzled by what was happening and might have believed their eyes were playing tricks. Where two human forms had been, after some obscure movements, there was one human and a large pale coloured beast whose pelt seemed to glow in the dim light reflected off the surface of the water.

The human scooped up handfuls of mud and plastered the wolf. Gradually the pale form vanished and a dark silhouette, barely visible in the poor light took its place. If the observer had looked away for a few moments, when next they looked, they would have been hard put to discern the two large wolf-like shadowy figures.

"It is done."

Muzzles touched.

"Remember, the dogs are the first consideration. From the sound of the barking they are big brutes. Be careful"

"You too. If you break through, keep on going. One of us must survive to bring word of these happenings to the Army Council. Phelan and his crew must be stopped before they do any more damage—McCrudden especially. He knows all about our forces and the names of those involved. He can't be allowed to worm his way back inside our organization again. He is a poisonous canker that has to be cut out."

● ● ●

"God almighty, what's that?" the soldier managed to blurt out, before the guard dogs went wild.

The strange howling was unearthly—somewhere out in the night, coming from one side and then from another direction entirely. It made the hairs on the neck curl and send prickles of fear down the spine. There was something primitive and unearthly about that sound. The voice of lost souls calling to the living to come and join them.

The soldiers, who had been stood down, awoke from their dozing, feeling little shivers of primitive fear. It was a fear born on the steppes of Europe when the world was young and man bore only primitive weapons to stave off the depredations of predators stronger and more ferocious than the puny creatures that walked on two legs. Endowed with fangs and claws, the wild beasts were formidable foes against which puny humans vied to protect themselves and their loved ones.

Now that same primeval fear had travelled thousands of years to the twentieth century and was causing men who were not normally religious to cross themselves and call upon their personal god to save them from the unnameable terror that stalked the night world of bog and loch and mud.

Maher stumbled from the back of the truck where he had been sleeping and dreaming of the hunt that was to come at dawn.

"What the hell is that?" he muttered, echoing the thoughts of every man it the camp.

His dogs were going wild, their vociferous barking mingling with the eerie howls coming out of the darkness.

"Secure the dogs!" he yelled suddenly, as he heard the cacophony of barking.

He had visions of his dogs breaking loose and streaking off into the night in pursuit of whatever phantoms were out there making that unearthly noise. He had no fear for the dogs' ability to survive any encounter with the creatures making that unholy howling, but he wanted to be with them to savour the kill when they tore the victim to pieces. The dog handler ran towards the picket lines.

The spikes hammered into the wet soggy earth were normally used to keep guy ropes secure. The force pulling on the ropes would be caused by wind beating on canvas walls and were more than adequate for that task. Against a mastiff, weighing more than a hundred pounds and hurtling itself against the restraint of the leather leash there was no contest. Some of the huge hounds broke free and raced out in a maddened frenzy to attack the beasts that dared encroach on the territory their master had set them to guard.

Maher managed to get to two of dogs in time to restrain them. But four sinister shapes streaked out into the night, crazed with bloodlust.

Averaging over one hundred pounds of muscle and gristle the dogs sped across the boggy ground seeking the interlopers. Their speed was awesome. Dark destroyers hurtling through the night; fangs glistening; lips curled back in anticipation.

Saliva leaked on their chests as the exhilaration of the hunt grew too intense to contain. They carried death in their fangs—snarling, vicious, painful death that awaited the foolish beasts that had strayed into their territory.

A dark mass with gleaming red eyes rose up to meet the rush. Joyously the leading dog hurled itself forward. Suddenly the target moved aside and swifter than a heartbeat a foreleg was snapped in two. Unable to stop the momentum the dog carried on running. The broken leg hit the ground and buckled. The dog tumbled as broken bone tore through skin and agony coursed through the animal. As it stumbled and went down, its snarling changed to pitiful howling. The dark shape pounced. It had the smell of the bog about it and the darkness of night. The noise ended abruptly as vicious fangs tore open the stricken brute's throat. It died instantly, the lifeless body flopping onto the dirt.

The attack dogs were still coming in and the second dog leapt high and hard for the wolf waiting patiently for the assault. With a movement too quick for the big dog to register, the black shape swept underneath. Keen fangs sliced open the animal's underbelly. The stricken dog tumbled to the ground. Valiantly it turned on its assailant but the black wolf ignored it and was positioning for the next attacker.

As the wounded dog tried to go after the big wolf, its feet became entangled in its guts dangling from the fearsome wound in its belly. Howling miserably the dog stumbled forward each step entangling the bloody intestines around it hind legs. It fell to the ground pawing at the dirt. A crushing weight descended on its back and powerful jaws closed on its neck biting into the spine and putting it out of its misery.

She turned and bounded over to where her partner was wrestling with the last two dogs. His powerful jaws had closed over the animal's snout cutting off its air supply. The black wolf was spinning around trying to keep the fourth dog from getting to grips.

Growling deep in its chest the hound struggled futilely to free itself of that deadly hold—legs scrabbling against the dirt, scuffing up tufts of grass and roots while its companion tried to get at the black shape that spun and dodged, always just out of reach. Too late it sensed the second dark shape. Something hard and brutal bowled it over. Before it could recover brutal fangs bit deep into its throat. Struggle as it might there was no breaking that deadly hold. The dog fought desperately but all too soon the fight went out of it as its blood poured from the lacerated throat. One final shake and the she wolf turned to watch her mate finish his victim.

The last dog was failing but still struggling. Nothing short of death would loosen the pressure the big wolf exerted as its fangs bit deep. It was ironic that the hound was about to end its life in a similar manner which it had doled out death to countless small mammals. Growling deep in its chest the hunting dog weakened, its struggles becoming feeble, until at last it ceased to thrash about and joined its companions in death.

• • •

Mather, with kicks and curses, eventually quietened the two dogs he had been able to hold on to. There was noise and disturbance from all around the camp as soldiers called out questions. No one knew what was happening. All was confusion until the officers shouted orders eventually restored order. An eerie silence descended. Men peered out into the darkness, seeing nothing of note and listening to the quiet of early morning. Phelan, using his hands as a megaphone, called his dogs in from the field.

"Lucifer, come on boy! Beelzebub, to me! Asmodai, good boy—to heel! Laldaboth, here boy!"

Again and again he called the dogs to which he had given demon's names, but there came no response. He was not to know his creatures of death and blood would hunt no more.

"Something's happened out there," he muttered.

He had a good idea what it was that had happened. His dogs had come upon the fugitives and attacked them. They were trained to kill. Even now they were probably feeding on the carcasses. The dog handler shivered. He was holding his two remaining animals with great difficulty as they strained to be let loose, their frustrated whining, the only sound in the night.

"It's not my bloody fault," he muttered. "I didn't want to come on this bloody jaunt in the first place."

CHAPTER THIRTY-TWO

"You there, dog fellow."

Major Bullock could not remember the wretched man's name, which didn't really bother him. His only interest in the Irish was to ascertain if they were rebels. Since he considered the vast majority of the Irish population to be backstabbing traitors he was suspicious of anyone who didn't express unequivocal loyalty to the British Crown.

"What the hell's happening?"

Mather cursed the two remaining dogs that were almost standing upright as they strained against their leads.

"Quiet you mongrels!" he yelled, before turning to the officer. "It's not my fault the dogs broke loose. Your men were supposed to keep them tied up. If they've killed those people you were hunting you can't blame me."

"What are you trying to tell me?"

"Look, mister, my dogs are trained to kill. That's what they are—hunting dogs. They're not housetrained mutts. When they broke loose and went out there after your fugitives, they did what they were trained to do. They're out there now standing over two dead bodies. Or if they ain't dead they'll be wishing they were."

"What the hell does that mean? And do not address me as mister. I am a major in the British Army. So address me as major or sir."

"It means my goddamn dogs could be feeding. I allow them to do that sometimes after a kill."

"Feeding? Good lord man, you mean... you mean they're... they're eating those poor bastards."

Maher did not reply, staring out into the night.

"Can't you recall the beasts? Surely if you trained them properly they'll come in for you."

"They won't come in. Like I say, meat is meat to them."

"Can't you go out and fetch them?"

"They could be anywhere out there. They're not answering when I call."

"What do you suggest?"

"Get your men to form a sweep line and walk out there. As soon as the dogs are spotted you call me and I go and gather them in. Warn your men not to approach them. Their blood will be up and they're liable to attack anyone coming near them. They'll be protecting their kill."

"Good God man. I wanted to catch those bastards and hang them. They murdered a whole squad of RIC fellows."

"Well, my dogs have probably saved you the bother. I need to pull them back in before they get the craving for human flesh. It might be too late already. It worries me they haven't responded to my calls. If they're not reined in there's a chance they might go wild and start hunting people."

Colonel Bullock stared with distaste at this disgusting man with his even more repulsive animals.

In any event, the discipline of the British Army took over, and a scrimmage line was deployed across the width of the moorland.

"The dogs are extremely dangerous, so on no account must you approach them," the major instructed the assembled soldiers. "On sighting them you will fire a couple of shots in the air. The dog handler will then come to you and secure the dogs. Stand absolutely still once you sight them. The fellow assures us the dogs will not attack unless provoked."

In truth the soldiers did not need the warning to stay clear of the dogs. They were making sure to steer well away from the two the dog handler had managed to retain. Snarling and struggling madly to break free, Maher was finding it difficult to control them. In the end he had to seek permission to lock the crazed animals inside one of the trucks.

At last the operation got underway. Slowly the skirmish line moved out into the bog, each man keyed up and alert, unaware of the eyes observing their progress.

"No dogs in the line," Raurí observed. "What do you think?"

They could hear the muted barking of the dogs locked inside the army truck.

"We should make a break for it now. They're making a sweep and boxing us in. The line is thinly spaced out. Without the dogs to warn them they won't see us until we're right up on them. If we're quick we stand a chance of getting past before they react. We have darkness and speed on our side."

"You're right. This could be our only chance. You swing well out to the left and I'll go right. All being well, we'll meet up the other side of the camp. I love you, Aishling. You come safe out of this."

Muzzles touched briefly. The two black shapes disappeared into the darkness.

●　●　●

Benedict Phelan watched the departing soldiers.

"Maher reckons the dogs have done for those two."

"Maybe this is a good time for us to sneak away," McCrudden suggested. "I'm fed up with this. I want a warm bed and a decent breakfast."

Phelan grinned at his lieutenant.

"Don't forget the addition of a hot woman to warm your bed."

McCrudden grinned back at his boss.

"Pity we didn't get to have a piece of that Aishling Maloney," he said wistfully. "What a waste. Lying out there, torn to pieces by those bloody hounds."

Out in the night there was a commotion as shots were fired followed seconds later by more. Neither saw the two dark shapes that streaked through the camp.

"What the hell! They've found something. Shall we wait and see. Give me some satisfaction to see Mac Cathail dead."

"I hope he suffered."

"I don't think being torn to pieces by a pack of dogs would be a particularly easy death. With a bit of luck he's still alive out there with his bollix ripped off."

They chortled, oblivious to the fact they were under observation.

"No," she was calling—pleading. "We are clear. Let's go."

"It is them: Phelan and McCrudden."

They had streaked through the line of soldiers almost swifter than the eye could follow. There had been shots but nothing had come near. Now they were inside the camp and Raurí sensed his old enemy nearby.

"You go on. Wait for me by the road."

And then he was moving away from her, honing in on the scent of his foe. She waited and wondered if she should follow. Another thought occurred to her. With a stealthy movement she crept among the army vehicles. Crawling underneath and chewing at pipes and wires leaving a tangled mess and moving to the next vehicle, the smell and taste of petrol strong in her mouth and nostrils. Indulging her mischievous side, by giving short yipping barks when she got to the truck in which the dogs were locked. The vehicle rocked as the dogs went berserk, throwing themselves at the doors.

"What the hell's wrong with them dogs?"

Phelan turned and stared with some annoyance at the source of the noise. A black shape was crouched nearby watching him.

"The goddamn things have escaped!" he yelled.

He stumbled back, fear stabbing his heart. The beast came off the ground at incredible speed and cannoned into Phelan's chest knocking him to the ground.

"Help me!"

A hot slavering mouth gaped above him and he could have sworn the beast spoke his name.

McCrudden could not get his limbs to move as he watched with fast beating heart the huge beast crouching over his boss. Terror griped his insides and he felt as if his heart was about burst from its mooring.

"Help me!" Phelan yelled again.

McCrudden wanted to help, but he could not stop shaking. The beast turned its head and looked at him. For a terrifying moment the glowing red eyes focused on McCrudden and his bladder vented.

McCrudden stumbled back a few paces. Those terrible glowing eyes remained focused on him and his trembling was so extreme he could hardly stand. With a cry he turned to run. Behind him Phelan's yells were suddenly cut short.

Sobbing, and calling on God and his holy saints to save him, McCrudden kept running. He didn't see the black shape appear in front of him. Too late his knees crashed into the solid bulk of the animal and he pitched helplessly forward tumbling over the obstruction and crashing to the ground.

A piece of the night parked on his chest, crushing what little wind he had left from his lungs. McCrudden tried to suck air into his labouring lungs and with it came the smell of petrol and earth and blood and an unidentifiable beastlike aroma.

"McCrudden," the beast whispered, the sounds, sibilant like a leaking tyre. "We had a date. I waited but when you did not turn up I thought I better come looking for you."

At that point McCrudden's heart gave out. The combination of the terror he was undergoing, along with the strain as his lungs battling for air against the compression of that terrible nightmare creature on his chest was all too much and McCrudden died of fright.

● ● ●

Maher stood aghast as he contemplated the scene of carnage. A soldier stood to one side holding a torch that cast flickering illumination over the ghastly scene. The bodies were sprawled untidily in the grass, the smell of blood and spilt intestines along with vented bowels and leaked urine was dense and overwhelming in the sharp night air.

"What could have done this?"

There was movement behind him and Major Bullock appeared out of the darkness.

"Bloody hell, man. Are those your dogs?"

"Of course they're mine, or what remains of them."

"Good God! The buggers fell to fighting and killed each other. What a bloody mess."

Phelan turned a bleak eye on the Englishman.

"No, they didn't bloody well kill each other. These dogs were part of a pack. Members of a pack don't turn on each other. This was something else—something big and powerful. It may well have been another pack.

When your men fired off those shots what did they see?"

"See! According to them it was dogs that ran past. They just run through the line. We assumed it was your beasts. This means the rebels are still out there." The major turned to his captain. "We still haven't caught the boogers. They're somewhere between here and that Lough. Get the lines moving again."

Leaving the dog handler mourning his dead animals, the soldiers continued their sweep of the bog. Nothing more was discovered as they moved through. Eventually the sound of waves lapping on the shore filtered through the night. The line of men stopped at the edge of the water. Someone shouted out and heads turned to the sound.

"What is it?"

"Clothes, sir—a bundle of clothing."

Major Bullock looked on while Captain Lawson examined the find. The captain held up some items of clothing.

"There are garments for both sexes. And a gun also. It must belong to them, Mac Cathail and his woman."

"They went in the Lough! Damn it, I was told no one could survive in those waters without a boat."

"Boogers must have been desperate. Bottled up here, with nowhere to go they must have taken the only way out. Maybe they knew they wouldn't make it. If they were desperate enough they might have thought that was their only option. If they were captured they faced hanging..."

The major let his words die away as he stared out at the choppy waters of the Lough.

"Either way the Lough probably did our job for us. Pity, I was looking forward to hanging that murderous pair."

• • •

A faint streak of red was edging into the sky not bringing enough light yet to distinguish details. The scattered rectangular shapes of the army vehicles hunkered on the boggy ground awaiting the return of the soldiers out in the bog searching for the fugitives. Except for the frantic barking of the dogs locked inside the army truck the camp was ominously quiet.

Clutching the steering wheel in knuckle-whitening grip, a very frightened man, along with his companions huddled in the cab of Benedict Phelan's lorry. From time to time they wiped the mist forming on the inside of the glass. Peering fearfully into the murk of the emerging dawn they tried not to look at the two bodies stretched out in the grass adjacent to the truck.

"Can you see anything?"

"Not a bloody thing."

They wiped furiously at the fog forming on the glass, scared the thing out there in the night would sneak up on them.

"What the hell was it?"

There was no answer for no one knew what it was that had come out of the night with dreadful glowing eyes and had settled upon the chest of the screaming Benedict. They had fought their way into the truck, punching and wrestling with each other in a mad scramble to get away from the terrifying apparition that had silently appeared out of the darkness.

"Start the goddamn truck. Let's get away from this place."

The starter whirred—the engine stuttered as if about to burst into life then died, the only sound the endless whining of a motor vainly trying to fire up an engine starved of fuel.

Out on the road, two dark shapes sat gazing back into the bog.

"We'd better go before they come after us."

"They won't be going anywhere."

Muzzles touched.

"You smell like a Model T Ford."

"Is that what it was? I had a job to get under it. The trucks were easy. Plenty of room underneath."

He looked to the red tinge in the sky.

"We'll have to go to ground before daylight proper. Our first priority will be to get some clothes."

"Where can we go? There'll be a price on our heads."

"Dublin. We'll need to report to the Army Council. They will look after us."

"Dublin, I've never been there. You went there and fought in the uprising."

"It seems I've done nothing but fight ever since."

They set off at an easy lope.

"Raurí, do you think there will ever be peace?"

THE END

ABOUT OUR CREATORS

AUTHOR --

PHILIP McCORMAC - is the author of nineteen BLACK HORSE WESTERNS, twelve as P.McCormac and seven using various pseudonyms. He has also published crime thrillers, historical thrillers, supernatural thrillers as well as short stories in various genres. Endeavour Media have published many of Philip's back-list as EBooks.
Website. www.PhilipMcCormac.co.uk

INTERIOR ILLUSTRATOR --

ROB DAVIS - began his professional art career doing illustrations for role-playing games in the late 1980s. Not long after he began lettering and inking, then penciling comics for a number of small black and white comics publishers—most notably for Eternity Comics (which eventually became Malibu Comics in the 1990's) on their book SCIMIDAR with writer R.A. Jones. Branching out to other black and white publishers and eventually working at both DC and Marvel Rob worked on likeness intensive comics like TV adaptations of QUANTUM LEAP as well as STAR TREK's many incarnations—mostly on the DEEP SPACE NINE comics for Malibu. At Marvel he worked on the Saturday morning cartoon adaptation PIRATES OF DARK WATER. After the comics industry implosion in the late 1990's Rob picked up work on video games, advertising illustration and T-shirt design as well as some small press comics like ROBYN OF SHERWOOD for Caliber. Rob continues to do the odd self-published comic book as well as publisher and designer for his small-press production REDBUD STUDIO COMICS. Rob is Art Director, Designer and Illustrator for the New Pulp production outfit AIRSHIP 27 partnered with writer/editor Ron Fortier. Rob is the recipient of the PULP FACTORY AWARD for "Best Interior Illustrations" in 2010, 2014, and 2016 for his work on SHERLOCK HOLMES: CONSULTING DETECTIVE and has been nominated for the same award every year since its inception. He works and lives in central Missouri with his wife and two children.
    For examples of his work surf the internet to: robmdavis.com

COVER ARTIST --

STEVE OTIS – started to draw at a very early age. Fueled by images of DC and Marvel comics. He soon discovered the great Warren magazines (Creepy and Eerie in the early 70's). From there he began to delve more deeply into horror, gothic and sci fi type art. Heavily influenced by Frazetta, Boris and Richard Corben, he began experimenting in oil paints in 1988.

Steve's first desire was to become a fantasy illustrator and did quite a bit of work in that style in the late 90's for CCG (collectible card games). By the early 2000's he started using exclusively acrylics. He began to look for techniques to challenge his artistic style in a more "Fine Art" vein while keeping a firm thematic of dark art.

Steve taught art in high school for 10 years before concentrating on painting. He has produced quality work as a comics artist, illustrator, and sculptor. Active as an artist since 1990 Steve began focusing his efforts in the world in fine (dark) art in 2005. Since then he has participated in many solo exhibitions and collective art shows in Quebec, Montreal, Italy and a few states in the USA.